Tragic

Mercy

Tragic Mercy

Book I

E. A. Owen

Twisted Karma
Publishing

Tragic Mercy: Book I
Previously Published as: A Curse Of Torment
Copyright © 2018 by Twisted Karma Publishing.

Cover Design: Ira-Rebeca (Ukraine)

Author Website: eaowenbooks.com
Facebook.com/eaowenbooks

For My Dear Friend KC
I wish life had turned out
differently for you
I miss you!

Tragic Mercy

PROLOGUE

The throbbing in my skull was so violent it felt like my head was splitting in two. Disoriented, drifting in and out of consciousness, my eyelids slowly fluttered open, blinded by the bright light. A loud ringing echoed through my ears. I felt like a helpless prisoner to the excruciating pain.

What just happened?

Raising my trembling hand, I wiped the warm liquid running down my forehead—it was blood. I gasped, feeling every ache and broken bone. I laid there terrified, my eyes frantically darting back and forth. With every breath I took, a sharp pain jabbed my lungs. Shattered glass was everywhere.

I remembered with horror that Natalie was in the car with me. Painfully, I turned my head toward her until I could see her lifeless body. Her hair was thick with blood, and her crystal-blue eyes stared blankly, clouded over with an emptiness that chilled me. I strained my eyes, looking closer for anything; a breath, a blink—but nothing. She just lay there, still and silent. I tried to yell her name, but no sound came out. Warm tears rolled down my cheeks. *This is just a dream. This is just a dream,* I repeated to myself. Hoping if I said it enough, it would be true.

I closed my eyes and let out the most agonizing scream.

Tragic Mercy

PART I

FAMILY MEMORIES

As I walk the endless streets among happy families smiling and laughing together, as if they have no cares in this world, my tears fall like rain. Life used to be simple. I used to be happy. Now, my reality is full of darkness, anger, guilt, and sadness all whipping around me like a fierce tornado. I can only watch helplessly while everything around me is destroyed

***

On March 11, 1955, Madeline and Mason had their first child, a healthy baby girl they named, Mary Elizabeth Walker. According to my mother's diary, I was the most beautiful baby they had ever seen. Born with a head full of dark hair and big, bright blue eyes, a tiny little nose, and rosy red cheeks. I was the perfect baby, very precious and delicate. My mother said she never knew she could love someone so much the first time she saw me.

Over the next few months, Mom and Dad were discussing how they didn't think Massachusetts was the best place to raise a family. They never thought in a million years they would move away from family and friends, but to them it was just not the right place, now that they had a new addition to the family who had changed their entire perspective of the world.

They researched and discussed where they thought would be best for their family and careers. They put the house up for sale right after my first birthday, knowing the house could possibly sit on the market for years before it sold. They loved the house but knew they could find the perfect home anywhere their hearts desired.

After six months of people coming in and out of our house interested in buying it, they finally got an offer they couldn't refuse and had to get serious about moving, because they only had about three months for all the paperwork to go through and for the new family to move in. They felt that a small town in the mid-west would be perfect to raise a family. After long nights lying in bed discussing the best options, they came to a final decision of the little town of Astoria, South Dakota, a quiet town surrounded by farmland but not too far from everything. It was only a few miles from the border of Minnesota and just ninety miles north of the biggest city in South Dakota, Sioux Falls, with a population of over 60,000.

They researched houses for sale in Astoria and were shocked by how cheap they were. They spoke to a realtor on the phone and arranged times to see a few houses out there. Then they purchased plane tickets. I stayed with my grandparents while they went exploring South Dakota. They looked at three houses right in town and another just on the outskirts of Astoria on Oak Lake. The houses in town were much cheaper and needed some work, but they fell in love with the house on Oak Lake. It had a long gravel driveway and a dock leading out to the lake. It was peaceful and quiet with not another house in miles, so they would have plenty of privacy. The house was a pale yellow two-story, four-bedroom ranch with plenty of land and a great view of the lake. This was the perfect spot—away from the east coast traffic, crime, and drugs—to raise a family. They put an offer on the house and were waiting to hear back from the realtor. The very next day my parents got the good news that their offer had been accepted and went to a local bank to fill out the paperwork for a home loan.

***

Three months later, we were all packed and on our way to our new home in Astoria, South Dakota, which had a population of 155 people–halfway across the country. Life there would be much different than our life in Boston, which had a population of over half a million. There were lots of tears shed over leaving family and friends behind, as well as the place they were both born and raised. But my parents embraced the big change in our lives and knew this was the best decision they had ever made—besides getting married and having me of course.

Both my parents started their new jobs within a couple of weeks after the move. The commute to and from work, a scenic and peaceful drive, was seamless compared to all the traffic in Boston they had experienced daily. I started daycare for the first time and loved playing with all the other kids my age and made lots of friends. But I missed my grandparents. I had gone to their house five days a week for almost fifteen months. I know all these little details because my mom kept a journal and shared with me all these wonderful details.

After a year in our new house and adjusting to our new lives out in the country, my mom announced that I was going to have a baby brother or sister soon. Her belly started getting bigger and my mom would grab my hand and put it on her tummy and ask me if I could feel the baby moving. I would lay my head on her belly and give the baby big hugs and lots of kisses.

***

A few weeks before my third birthday, my baby brother, Matthew Joseph, was born. We were a very happy family. All four of my grandparents came to visit us to meet my new baby brother, and while they were with us, we celebrated my third birthday. My parents threw a big princess birthday party for me and I got lots of presents! One set of grandparents stayed for a week and the other for a whole month to help my mom while Dad went back to work. I was sad to see them leave. I wanted them to stay with us forever, but once they left the house was quiet again.

My baby brother slept a lot. It made me sad because I wanted to play with him all the time, but he was too little to do anything fun. He just lay there. Soon enough, however, he started crawling and getting into everything. He would pull things down and knock things over. He thought it was funny and would laugh. Matthew had the cutest little laugh.

At six months old, Matthew started crawling. At least now I could chase him around the room. He tried to get away from me and was a fast-little bugger. Mom and Dad said it would probably be another five or six months before he would start walking.

I liked helping Mom feed him when he was old enough to sit in his highchair. I would climb into a chair next to him and copy what my mom did, swirling the spoon up and down and all around like an airplane while making funny noises until Matthew opened his mouth wide for a bite. He made a big mess when he started eating, all over his face and on his bib, and I'm sure I didn't help much, being only three and a half years old at the time, but I loved being Mommy's little helper. It made me feel like a big girl.

Matthew started walking before his first birthday and we used to clap and cheer him on with every step he took. It was a big deal for Mom. She missed all the firsts with me because she went right back to work when I was just twelve weeks old. She didn't want to miss any of it with Matthew, so my mom stayed at home and raised us after Matthew was born. My dad worked a lot, but we spent every weekend together and did fun stuff as a family and took lots of trips together.

For Matthew's first birthday, we went to the Lincoln Children's Zoo in Nebraska. We saw lots of animals, big and small, but our favorite was the monkeys, swinging around from tree to tree and making funny noises. We got to feed llamas, goats, and deer; and Matthew snuck some of their food in his mouth and ate it. Neither of our parents saw, and I just giggled and said, "EWWWW!" Mom and Dad were preoccupied by all the cool animals and they hadn't even noticed. Matthew didn't spit it out, so he must have liked it. To me, the animal food smelled bad and looked funny, but I found out at a young age that boys often do gross things. We spent all day at the zoo and stayed the night at a big hotel with a swimming pool. Dad had started teaching me how to swim when I was three. Matthew was still too little, but he liked dunking his head under the water and getting all wet and we laughed and splashed each other a lot.

We had a little party at the hotel with cake and presents. Matthew was old enough to rip open all the presents by himself. He ripped them apart fast, then threw the gift aside and went to the next. Mom tried picking up each gift and telling him all about it, but he wasn't interested. He just wanted to open the next, and the next, and so finally she stopped trying. My mom said I was the complete opposite. I wanted to start playing with each gift I opened and kept forgetting that I had more. So, Mom would have to take the gift away and hide it behind her back and put a newly wrapped gift in front of me.

My brother's favorite present was the big dinosaur that roared and moved on its own. Matthew loved dinosaurs! His favorite blanket had dinosaurs all over it. After Matthew was done opening all his gifts, Mom said she had a surprise to tell all of us, even Dad. She told us she was pregnant, and we were going to have another baby brother or sister. My dad gave my mom a kiss. My parents were very affectionate and weren't afraid to show it. We were a very happy family and always laughed a lot and played together.

Just six weeks after Matthew's first birthday, we took a trip to the Black Hills of South Dakota. My dad had always wanted to see Mount Rushmore, and now that we lived in South Dakota it was the perfect opportunity. We also got to go to Reptile Gardens. My favorite part was riding on the giant tortoise. Matthew loved all the different types of snakes. He was fascinated by them.

On our way back to the hotel, we picked up pizza. My favorite topping was pepperoni. Matthew had only cut a few teeth, and so Mom had to cut his into tiny pieces, so he didn't choke—but he loved pizza too.

We celebrated my birthday as soon as we got back home with cake and ice cream. I invited a few friends over for a sleepover. After I opened all my presents, we laid everyone's sleeping bags, side-by-side, on the floor in the living room. We stayed up until midnight, painting our nails, doing our hair, and putting on makeup. Mom said we looked like clowns. My mom even let me put makeup on her too. I was so proud of myself. I don't think she liked it too much, but she laughed and knew I was having fun.

In March my other baby brother, Michael Alan, was born. He was much smaller than Matthew, only weighing four pounds and five ounces. He was born eight weeks early due to complications during my mom's pregnancy.

Michael couldn't come home right away. So we visited him every day in the hospital for six weeks until he was strong enough to come home with us. It made Mom sad that he had to stay in the hospital, but I was too young to really understand what was going on at the time. When Michael finally came home, he cried all the time. Dad asked me to be on my best behavior and help out Mom as much as I could since she wasn't getting much sleep at night and had a lot on her plate.

Being just four years old, I was very confused by what my dad was trying to say, and so, responded by saying, "But Mom's sleeping; she doesn't have anything on her plate."

My dad just chuckled, rubbed my head and replied, "What I meant sweetheart, is your mom has a lot to do and needs you to be a big girl and help her out, especially with Matthew. You've got to keep an eye on him and stay quiet so your mom can rest."

"Okay, Daddy," I replied. Dad leaned down on one knee, gave me a kiss on the cheek, then wrapped his arms around me in a big bear hug, stood up and swung me around as I giggled.

"I know you will sweetie, but Daddy's got to leave for work, so please remember our little talk."

My dad left, and it was just the four of us. I really hoped that Michael wouldn't cry all day again—it hurt my ears.

I looked up to my father dearly. I was the typical Daddy's Girl. My father could do no wrong in my eyes. I hoped one day to meet a man just like him, a prince charming to sweep me off my feet.

After Michael was born, Mom changed. She wasn't as happy anymore. She was tired all the time and didn't play with Matthew and me much anymore. So I tried to stay quiet and play with Matthew so Mom could tend to our baby brother who never seemed happy. All he did was sleep and cry. I used to ask Mom why he cried all the time, but she didn't know either. In fact, we had to go to the doctor a lot because Mom wanted to find out what was wrong with Michael and if he would ever stop crying. Then one day I overheard Mom and Dad talking in the kitchen while Matthew and I were playing with toys in the other room. I could hear my mom crying and my dad kept saying everything was going to be okay. It wasn't until months later that I found out what was wrong and why Mommy had been so sad and cried. Michael had been diagnosed with cancer. He had a tumor and was in pain all the time, which explained his constant crying. I didn't know how serious this was, or what it even meant. All I knew was that it was bad because it made Mom and Dad very sad and we had to go to the doctors all the time to make Michael better.

Michael had to stay in the hospital for a long time, and we visited him every day. The doctors told Mom that Michael would get better, and he wouldn't be in so much pain anymore, and I was hoping that meant he would stop crying too. I wanted us to be a happy family again, and that meant making my baby brother better. The doctors caught the cancer before it spread, and after Michael recovered from the surgery, he was able to be a normal kid, which meant no more crying, which made us all very happy.

After what happened to Michael, however, Mom and Dad were scared to have any more children. Even though Michael was all better, they still worried all the time. Anytime Michael showed the slightest hint of getting sick, my mom would rush him to the doctor to make sure it was nothing serious. She was in fact very paranoid, but every time the doctors would reassure her that he was okay and there was nothing to worry about. She was told he was just sick like any other kid and that she had to stop worrying so much. She was told he was healthy and the chances of a tumor coming back were very slim. But my mom still worried all the time, but I don't blame her. She didn't want anything bad happening to us; we were everything to her.

After Michael's illness, I realized it taught me a very important concept that I desperately needed later in life. For instance, how adversity is overcome, how loved ones react, and how they pull together in difficult situations. The experience has tattooed my soul and I am all the stronger for the psychological trauma of afflictions that I would later in life come to suffer severely.

***

Finally, life was normal again. Mom didn't go to the doctor's every time Michael coughed or sneezed or had a fever. She started treating him like Matthew and me, and we went on family trips again, laughed, and played together. We were a happy family again. That is, until I was seven, Matthew was four, and Michael three. Mom found out she was pregnant again and was scared because of what Michael had been through as a baby. She didn't want to go through that stress and heartache again, which made this pregnancy not a happy one like all the others—and she felt guilty that she wasn't happy but scared all the time.

Only a few weeks after finding out she was pregnant, it all turned for the worse. Dad was at work and the four of us were sitting on the couch together watching a movie, Michael sitting in Mom's lap. I remember because she almost threw him off her when she stood up, grabbed her stomach, and let out a bloodcurdling scream. I was horrified. I had no idea what was wrong with her. She ran into the kitchen and picked up the phone and called my dad at work and told him to hurry home because something was very wrong. After hanging up the phone, she slowly slid down the cabinets and sat on the floor. I ran to her to see if she was okay, and tears were streaming down her face while she held her belly. She told me to go back in the living room and watch the movie with my brothers. She said that she was going to be okay and that Dad was on his way home. I did as she told me but peeked around the corner when I saw her crawling to the bathroom on her hands and knees. She closed the door behind her, and I could hear her sobbing from the hallway. This made me very sad and scared.

I just sat on the couch, trying to watch the movie, but I couldn't focus. I was sitting on the edge of the couch biting my nails, not knowing what was wrong with Mom. Matthew and Michael hadn't seemed to notice what was going on, their eyes glued to the TV screen. I snuck away from the living room, tiptoed down the hall to the bathroom where my mom was hiding and put my ear up to the door; but I couldn't hear anything.

She wasn't crying anymore, and so I quietly asked, "Mom, are you okay?" She didn't answer. "Mom! MOM!" Still nothing, so I slowly turned the doorknob, hoping she hadn't locked it. I pushed the door open and she was lying on the floor, unconscious. I got down beside her and shook her shoulder, repeating over and over again, "Mom, wake up, wake up!"

I started to panic. I didn't know how long it would be before Dad got home, but then he came rushing through the door—yelling.

"Madeline, where are you?"

I spoke up. "Dad, Mom's in here!"

He came running down the hall, panic on his face.

"What's wrong with your mom?" Dad softly asked me.

"I don't know, but she won't wake up!" I replied.

He told me to go get my brothers and meet him out in the car.

As my dad carried my mother out to the vehicle, she looked lifeless, her head hanging down. I remember being scared and wondering if my mom was even alive. My dad laid her in the passenger's seat and leaned it back, so she wouldn't fall forward as he drove. After he buckled her safely in, he made sure all of us were in the car and secured in our seatbelts, then sped off to the hospital in Hendricks, Minnesota, the closest hospital to our house.

My dad must have been going 80 mph the entire way to the hospital, and the trip didn't take us long at all.

Waiting for the doctor to come out and tell us if Mom was going to be okay seemed like eternity, and my father kept pacing back and forth nervously while my brothers were playing with the toys in the waiting room. I didn't want to play. I just sat in a chair with my hands folded in my lap, patiently waiting for the news. When the doctor finally came out, my dad rushed over to him and he quietly told my father what was wrong with my mother. They talked for a few minutes and then the doctor turned away and walked through the doors. My father came over to me and told me to keep an eye on my brothers because he needed to go see Mom. I just nodded and dropped my head down while he walked away. I glanced over to make sure my brothers were still playing in the same spot, which they were, as quiet as could be. Dad must have been in there for twenty minutes before he came back to check on us, and we were all in the same exact places as when he left. He came over and kneeled in front of me.

"Mom is going to be okay, but she needs to rest for a while. Let's go home. We can come back and visit her later, after she has had time to rest."

I didn't find out until years later what really happened to Mom that day. My parents kept telling me that I was too young to understand, that it was complicated. They just told me that Mom had lost the baby and she was lucky to be alive. I was confused. How she could lose the baby, which was in her tummy? They had to explain to me that the baby died, and Mom would not be able to have any more children.

But that wasn't the case at all. A year later my mom was pregnant again, but she was skeptical after what the doctor told her when she miscarried almost a year before. My parents were very scared this time. Mom saw the doctor a lot in the beginning to make sure everything was okay. After every appointment they were reassured that the baby was healthy and growing properly.

Once my mom started showing, it wasn't necessary to go to the doctor as often anymore and she only went to regular, scheduled appointments. Mom and Dad called the baby their "Miracle Baby" and informed us it was a baby girl. Now I would have a baby sister, and that made me excited! At first, they were going to call her Michelle, but at the last minute they changed their minds and named her Angelina Hope because she was their Angel of Hope. I was nine when she was born. My mom got her tubes tied this time. I wasn't sure what that meant at the time, but the doctors reassured them that they were lucky this time and that may not be the case the next. Besides, my parents said four kids was the perfect number for them. They were very grateful we were all happy and healthy, and that's all that mattered.

***

For Angel's second birthday, my parents took us to Disneyland. I was eleven, Matthew was eight, and Michael seven. It was the best vacation ever! Dad took a whole week off from work and we all got to fly on an airplane for the first time.

We stayed in a log cabin for the week. It had two floors with a loft, and we had it all to ourselves. It was like being at home, including a kitchen with dishes, silverware, cookware, a washer and dryer, and even a massive stone fireplace and a Jacuzzi. I wanted to live here forever. What would be better than having Disneyland practically in our backyard. We went on tons of rides. I swear we stood in line waiting most the trip, but it was well worth it. We kept bugging our parents to tell us when we were coming back, and they said not for a long, long time since this was a very expensive trip and took almost all of their savings. But that was the last trip we would ever take with our parents again.

MARY

Eight Years Later

My parents were killed by a drunk driver when I was twelve. The man that killed my parents was from a wealthy, powerful family in South Dakota. The charges were dropped to vehicular manslaughter and he was sentenced to ten years in prison, all but thirty-six months suspended. After only serving thirty months, just two and a half years, he was released. My life and the lives of my three younger siblings were ruined forever because of him. We had to learn how to cope daily with neither of our parents in our lives. They will miss birthdays, Christmases, graduations, weddings, and the births of their grandchildren. Over the years, I grew so much hatred for this man, Lance Conrad, who took my parents' lives and only had to spend two and a half years in prison. He got to come out free as a bird and continue living his life as if nothing had changed, and this made my blood boil. I grew very angry and bitter towards him, towards the system, and towards the world. My parents didn't deserve this; we didn't deserve this. We are good people.

After doing some serious digging using a few connections, I discovered that Lance Conrad had a rap sheet a mile long, including a history of violence and drunkenness. He was charged with several counts of assault with a deadly weapon, public intoxication, statutory rape, DUI, drug possession, theft, and manslaughter. This information was not easy to get since his family had money and paid to have his criminal record covered up. He had a blood alcohol level of .32 the night he killed my parents, four times the legal limit. He walked away from the accident with only a broken nose, two black eyes, and a cracked rib. I was told he must have been unconscious when he swerved into their lane at 65 mph.

My parents' car was unrecognizable. There was no way they could have ever survived. The hood was completely crushed to the back seats because the car rolled several times before landing on the hood. My parents had been completely crushed in the car. The police said they'd died on impact, that they didn't feel a thing, but that didn't make it any easier to deal with. And no one was to blame except Lance Conrad, a 23-year-old boy who left a party drunk out of his mind and should have been in a coma, not behind the wheel of a car. That night forever changed our lives and was only the beginning of the cruel, twisted events that were to unfold.

***

In South Dakota it is not out of the ordinary for gusts of winds to reach 60 mph, making cold days seem much colder. Today was especially cold, with a bite to it that sent chills to the bone. In the winter, temperatures can drop double digits into the negatives, with a wind chill of fifty degrees below zero. It takes some getting used to, but to be honest, I don't think time will ever make these cold, windy days bearable to even those who have spent their entire lives here. It can be brutal.

I was taking classes at South Dakota State University aka SDSU, home of the Jackrabbits and our colors are yellow and blue. I was going to school to become a Registered Nurse, just like my mother. I really missed her and sometimes wondered what life would have been like if both my parents were still alive. My grandparents did a great job raising us, and both my parents had life insurance policies, the benefits divided equally among the four of us children. My grandparents set up a savings account for each of us with the money that we could access once we were eighteen. Let's just say it was a lot of money and will do some good, as long as we spend it wisely.

I waited at the crosswalk for a car to drive by before I walked across the street, both arms wrapped tightly around my upper body to try to keep warm. I ran across the street so fast with my head down to keep the wind from burning my face that I didn't even notice the curb and tripped. I caught myself with my hands and stood up quickly, hoping no one had seen me fall, just as I felt fingers tap the back of my shoulder.

"Are you okay?" a deep voice from behind me asked with concern.

"Yeah, I'm fine," I said embarrassed, feeling my face flush as I turned around. I'd never seen him before. I would certainly have remembered if I had; you don't ever miss a face like that. He was tall with a square jaw and deep-set eyes that were mesmerizing. He appeared to be muscular, but it was hard to tell for sure with a big, bulky jacket on.

"My name is Elliott, and it's nice to meet you," he said, holding out his hand.

"I'm Mary," I replied, and taking his hand in mine I noticed his strong grip, my gaze lasting a bit longer than normal. He was very attractive, and I couldn't help but smile ear to ear as I blushed, shyly looking down at the ground.

"Are you headed to class?" Elliott asked.

"Yes, yes I am," I replied

"You mind if I walk you to class? I would hate for you to lose your balance again. Maybe my arm would be of some assistance," he said, smirking.

"Are you making fun of me?" I asked playfully.

"Maybe a little, but you're cute when you're embarrassed!" he said, grinning. I couldn't help but look away. His confidence and good looks were intimidating. "And maybe after class you could show me around town. I'm new to the area and could use some help from a pretty little lady like yourself to keep me company." All I could think of was how hypnotic his eyes were. It was like he had me in a trance, and I couldn't speak. After a few moments, he spoke up to void the silence that fell between us. "But if you're busy later, maybe some other time would work better for you?"

"Ummm, yeah, I get out of class at 4:00. Where would you like to meet?" I asked him shyly.

"Why don't I pick you up here, and we could grab a bite to eat and get to know each other a little better?" His voice was deep and very sexy. "I'll park out front and wait for you there. I wouldn't want you to blow away on me before I get the chance to dazzle you with my charm," He said playfully and with a smile. I just stood there, speechless, dumbfounded by how confident, sexy, and playful he was—and he knew he had me. "I will take that as a yes."

"Sorry, you ah, just caught me off guard. Guys around here are shy and beat around the bush. I'm just not used to this is all," I replied.

"I will take that as a compliment, and I will let you get to class before you are late. I will see you at 4:00. I drive a black Lexus," he said as he turned away.

The whole time in class I couldn't concentrate. My attention kept going back to Elliott, that deep voice, his eyes, his confidence. He was a very beautiful man with a sexy smile that would make any girl's heart melt. Standing at 5ft 10in, 140lbs with long, straight blonde hair that fell a few inches past my shoulders, big, emerald green eyes and a few freckles that kissed my nose and cheekbones, I was far from the most attractive girl around. I barely wore any makeup compared to most of the girls my age, who mostly cake it on and look fake. I have been told I have natural beauty and only wear a little makeup to brighten my pale skin, but I am shy and not very social. I pretty much keep to myself. Some call it stuck up but I'm far from conceited. I just don't like the drama that young adults my age bring. I try to keep my life very simple and as uncomplicated as possible.

I have enough money from the trust fund to live off very well, but I don't flaunt it like most people would. I don't want friends or boyfriends just because I have money. I want true friends who are there because they truly care. But unfortunately, society is very selfish and money-driven, and I don't want to be a part of that. I didn't know what Mr. Charming saw in me, but I was happy we ran into each other and that he wanted to get to know me better. A guy like that will make you forget all your worries for a while. I only met him for a few minutes, but there was something about him that was so tantalizing and made my entire body tingle in excitement. All I could do was daydream about him, and you couldn't wipe the stupid grin off my face.

Four o'clock came around faster than I had expected. I grabbed my books, realizing I hadn't heard a thing the professor said during the entire class because I was busy daydreaming, which is not like me at all. I always pay attention and takes notes. My only priority was getting good grades so I could graduate college and obtain my nursing degree. Now, after meeting Elliott, my focus was on him entirely, how dreamy he looked and that voice, so deep and sexy. How could someone have that kind of effect over me in just a few minutes? I knew I might want to steer clear of him if I intended to graduate in the next couple years. Otherwise my mind might be off in La La Land and not focused on homework or studying.

As I walked outside, I peered across the parking lot, looking for a black Lexus. I saw headlights flash on and off a few hundred feet in front of me, but the fog made it hard to see since during class it had grown to a thick mist. At least the wind had died down for now. As I walked across the parking lot, I became very self-conscious. I hadn't had time to even look in the mirror or freshen up, and I was beginning to feel nervous at the thought of being around him. What if he thought I was boring and wanted nothing to do with me? What if I was at a loss for words? I was starting to second guess myself and to clam up before I even reached his car. I could turn back now and forget I even met Elliott in the first place, but there was something drawing me to him, a magnetic force that I couldn't resist. It was a feeling I'd never felt before, and it was scary and exciting all at the same time.

What was it about him? I just couldn't put my finger on it, but there was no turning back now. As I approached his car, the driver's door flew open and he came strolling around the front of the car to the passenger's side and opened the door for me. He spoke in that low, sexy voice, "Mary, it's nice to see you again." A confident, wide grin stretched across his face, his eyes captivating me.

"Hi, Elliott," I shyly replied as I crouched to get into his car. He shut the door behind me. It smelled new, with a mixture of whatever cologne he had on, which was very seductive and manly smelling. As he climbed in the driver's seat, he glanced over at me with a sparkle in his eyes that made him irresistible.

"Did you decide where we should grab a bite to eat?" I looked away almost immediately. His gaze made me more nervous than I had imagined it could.

"I was thinking someplace quiet with good food, possibly Bravo's, which is just a few blocks away. The place is usually hopping on the weekends, but it should be quiet enough tonight, it being Monday and all."

"I like that. Most women I come across tend to leave all the decisions to me. I like a woman who knows exactly what she wants and doesn't second guess herself." His response made me blush instantly.

The last date I had been on was about nine months ago. His name was Adam, and he was cute and nice enough, but we just didn't hit it off. We went on a few dates, but nothing came of it, probably because he had a few too many to drink one night while we were out, and things got a little hot and heavy and I didn't feel comfortable sleeping with him. He was very pushy and made me feel uncomfortable. I told him no, but he was persistent, and reeked like a brewery. He was slurring his words and couldn't stand up straight; it was an immediate turn off. Don't get me wrong, I like to drink, but after a couple glasses of wine and I'm good. I don't like the feeling alcohol gives me when I have a few too many, especially the next morning—I hate hangovers. Finally, I'd had enough of his drunken behavior. I told him I had to go to the ladies' room and I never came back. Rumors went around campus like a wildfire that I was an uptight bitch who didn't know the first thing about having fun and that I left Adam stranded without a ride.

A few guys have asked me on dates since, but I turned them all down. One of them was so offended that he told me that the rumors were right about me and walked away. Guys my age were immature and partied too much, and that's not the type of man I wanted to settle down with. I had more important things to worry about than dating.

And then Elliott came along and changed my way of thinking completely. Just then my door opened and all I could see was Elliott's hand reaching out for mine. "What a gentleman!" I said as I grabbed his hand. He just smiled and we walked up to the restaurant hand in hand. Nothing felt more right. During the entire dinner conversation, he made me feel at ease and there were no awkward silences. It felt natural to be with him, and better yet, he was easy on the eyes. I could see myself falling for him hard, and at that moment I knew we would spend the rest of our lives together.

ELLIOTT

Sixteen Years Later

How did my life turn upside down so abruptly? How did I not see the warning signs? Or did I and subconsciously ignored them because I didn't want to believe that this perfect world I thought we'd created was a lie. I could not ask for more. I had a loving husband, a beautiful daughter, the perfect job and home. I didn't want to believe the devastating news, but it was all so very real and brought about complete and utter destruction. As much as I wish I could take away the pain and betrayal of trust my daughter has extensively experienced, there is no going back into time to fix this horrific anomaly. Where to begin?

I fell deeply, madly in love with Elliott Hamlin. I was just twenty years old. We made love. He proposed to me. I found out I was pregnant. We got married six months later, and just three short months following our wedding, our baby girl, Natalie, was born. Elliott was a very loving, attentive, respectful husband and father. He reminded me a lot of my own father. We took many family vacations together to Hawaii, Germany, Italy, Rome, Norway, Iceland, New Zealand... You name it, we've been there.

We lived a life full of luxury and happiness. But Elliott was having an affair that I was unaware of, and my precious daughter got caught in the middle. She loved her father dearly and unconditionally, keeping secrets for him. How heavy a burden that must have been to keep all those secrets bottled up and no one to turn to. If she had just told me, maybe I could have stopped this whirlwind of events that have destroyed this family. But as a child, it was not her responsibility. It was her father's secrets and his betrayal that destroyed everything, and he was solely responsible for his actions.

My life was too good to be true, and maybe Elliott overcompensated for his lies and secrets by being the most loving and affectionate man. I never once second guessed his intentions. I trusted him completely. I just thought I was the luckiest woman in the world to find such an amazing man to share my life. I have heard horror stories of men who are abusive and was happy that my Elliott was not one of them. But truth be told, he had been having an affair for years. It started with him working late, until 10:00, then progressively getting later and later, not getting home until after midnight some nights. But this only happened once or twice a week and he had legitimate reasons, or so I thought.

Then he got laid off from his job three years ago and had to be sneakier about his affair. He stayed at home with Natalie while I worked. I got promoted and started taking business trips a few times a year that lasted four to five days. Some trips I had to take lasted a week and sometimes two. During these times, Elliott got his friend, Joseph, to stay with Natalie while he would spend those days I was away with his girlfriend, Ashley.

The business trips after my promotion was when everything changed for the worse. I just assumed my husband was at the house when I was working and Natalie at school. But Elliott used my business trips, and trust, as a gateway to his affair without getting caught. When I came home from my business trips, the house would be clean, the laundry folded and put away, and the yard mowed; and my husband and daughter had stories of everything they had done while I was gone, like going out to eat or ordering in a pizza and watching movies together, or going out to the theater to see a new movie that was playing. They seemed very happy every time I came home, and I assumed it was because they got to spend quality time together and Natalie was absolutely a daddy's girl and loved spending time with him. In truth, Elliott was happy because he was banging a girl in her early twenties, but Natalie was hiding a deep, dark secret even from her dad.

To make a long story short, Elliott's affair resulted in him committing suicide, our daughter pregnant with twins at the age of fourteen, and his so-called friend, Joseph, in prison for molesting and raping our daughter for three years. This was devastating to our family. Things will never be the same again. Natalie has to grow up without a father and with the mental and emotional damage from the rape. Natalie was in therapy, and we agreed that being a teenage mom with twins to remind her daily of being raped and the suicide of her father was not possible. Natalie had her whole life ahead of her. Abortion was out of the question, and so adoption was the only logical choice.

***

To My Beautiful Wife,

I am so sorry for what I have done. I cannot live with the guilt a day longer. The guilt has tormented my soul and I am reminded of how horrible a man I am every time I look at you and our daughter. I never meant for any of this to happen. I met Ashley at work when she was twenty-two and an assistant at the firm, and I eventually gave in to temptation and couldn't stop my sexual urges. I was not honest with you about being laid off. I resigned after the firm found out about Ashley since the relationship was considered against company policy. I was very selfish, and I blame myself for everything that has happened. The guilt is eating me alive. I can't eat or sleep. It is completely consuming me. I trusted Joseph to care for our daughter while I slept with another woman against our vows of marriage and I know this must hurt you immensely. But worst of all, the man I trusted raped our daughter for three years and got her pregnant. Even though Joseph was found guilty and is in prison for hurting our little girl, I cannot live with the guilt any longer. I am reminded of the horrible husband and father I am and how neither of you deserved this. So I am doing what I do best and being selfish by ending the torment that has been eating me alive. I am sorry for everything. You and Natalie will be much better off without me around. You both deserve a better man in your lives. I always loved you, Mary, even if you don't want to believe me. Goodbye, Elliott

***

I noticed that my daughter was more quiet than normal and wasn't acting herself for the last few years, but I assumed it was hormones and the transition of becoming a teenager and all the stress from school and homework. I never thought she was being raped in our home by a man I only met a few times. I blame myself for being so naive and not taking my daughter's behavior changes seriously. Now I drown myself in what-ifs. What if I hadn't been promoted, for example? I would have never had to go on business trips and my husband wouldn't have asked his friend to stay with our daughter, alone and overnight, so he could sneak off and have an affair. I, of course, noticed we hadn't been having as much sex as we used to, that our love life was dwindling away, but I just assumed it was because we had been married for so long. I never thought he would cheat on me. I trusted him without a doubt. I thought we were happy. I thought we had the perfect life together. We took lavish vacations every year. We had a big, beautiful house and nice cars. Elliott was always very loving and attentive to me and our daughter. Natalie adored her father and I was madly in love with my husband. We had everything!

I took a leave from work to be with my daughter during this horrific time in our lives. She was having a really hard time dealing with the death of her father and the hormonal and physical changes from the pregnancy. We both were going to therapy to deal with the tragedy that had changed our lives forever. I don't know how much it helped, but at least it gave us the opportunity to speak to a professional openly about what we were going through emotionally. And Natalie could tell her therapist things she might be afraid to tell me, or not feel comfortable telling me, because maybe deep down inside she blames me for all this happening to our family. Natalie was also having a very difficult time at school. Kids can be so cruel!

***

I was in the laundry room just finishing up folding the last few items in the dryer when I heard the door open and then close, followed by a click. I could hear Natalie crying but it sounded muffled. "Sweetheart, is everything okay?" I asked while I walked down the hall that led to the living room, feeling the hardwood floor against my bare feet as I walked. Natalie was curled up on the floor next to the front door with her hands covering her face while she sobbed uncontrollably. "Honey, what happened?" I sat down beside her, rubbing her back to try to comfort her. I could tell she was trying to calm herself down. I remained silent, waiting for her to tell me when she was ready. The worst thing to do is to try to rush her into telling me because I can never understand what she is saying when she is crying like this. I continued rubbing her back, praying it was just her pregnancy hormones getting the best of her and that it was nothing serious.

As we sat there on the floor for a few minutes, Natalie finally got hold of herself and lifted her head. Her eyes were filled with tears, her cheeks streaked from the tears rolling down them. She looked so vulnerable and innocent that I just wanted to grab her and hug her tight and never let go, telling her everything was going to be okay. But instead, I gave her space because I knew that she would just breakdown crying again. "The kids at school called me a slut." Natalie took a deep breath. "They said I was such a disappointment to my father that he killed himself!" She started bawling again, this time having a hard time breathing and so started hyperventilating.

I just wrapped my arms around her and gave her a big hug while she cried on my shoulder. "Natalie, honey, kids say some very cruel things, but let me just tell you this: they are ignorant because they don't know the situation and the awful things you have been through. If only they knew, and of course it's none of their business, they would be comforting you and being kind, not saying these horrible things about you or to you. This was not of your fault. You are just a child, and no kid should have to go through what you have. And I'm so sorry I wasn't here for you to stop this from happening. I'm your mom and I should have known something very wrong was going on and I feel guilty for not doing anything about it." I felt a big lump forming in my throat and it became difficult to speak.

"Mom, don't blame yourself. You had no idea, and neither did Dad. I wasn't honest with you about Dad being gone while you were away on your business trips and Joseph staying here with me. I kept secrets from you, and I kept this secret from Dad too. And because I didn't tell either of you what Joseph was doing to me, Dad killed himself." Natalie began to cry uncontrollably again and buried her face into me even deeper while I rubbed the top of her head.

"Sweetheart, do not ever blame yourself for what your father did. It is no one's fault but Joseph's, and he is in prison, being punished for hurting you." We sat silently on the floor for quite some time until Natalie broke the silence.

"Mom, I'm really hungry. I didn't eat lunch at school because I was too upset. Could we go to Guajajara's for dinner? I'm really craving Mexican right now, and we could share a fried iced cream for dessert."

"Of course we can, sweetheart. Let me grab my purse and we'll head right over. I'll meet you in the car."

Dinner was delicious, but we always got disgusted looks every time we go out because my teenage daughter was pregnant. At first it bothered me, and I just wanted to yell at everyone, "What are you looking at? It's not what you think! My daughter was raped by a sick man who is in prison and this is not her fault, so mind your own damn business and leave us be!" But now I just ignore the awkward glances and encourage my daughter not to pay any attention to them, but that is always easier said than done. We stayed home as much as possible when she first started showing, which was sooner than most since she was pregnant with twins, because the looks and whispers bothered us so much. It was unbearable at first, but time has made it easier and we don't let them ruin our time out anymore because we are no longer afraid of what other people think. My daughter deserves to live her life and not feel like she has to hide from everyone. She has been through enough.

We went to Natalie's OB appointment after school the following Wednesday afternoon. She was eight months pregnant now and her belly was huge. Natalie was a tiny girl, standing at 5ft 6in tall and 95 lbs, before the pregnancy. She has long, honey brown hair that reaches the middle of her back and big crystal-blue eyes. The doctor informed us that the babies were healthy and growing perfectly. This is usually a time to be happy, but it was just a reminder of the horrible things that man did to my daughter. Natalie decided not to find out the sexes of the babies since they were being put up for adoption and she thought the less she knew about them the easier it would be.

NATALIE

Summer vacation was just around the corner, and Natalie was ecstatic. She was having a very difficult time dealing with all the rumors going around about her in school. She did a pretty good job hiding it, for the most part, but I could read, deep into her eyes, that she was hurting a great deal and didn't want to upset me. We had just finished eating Natalie's favorite, lasagna and cheesy garlic bread, for dinner at the breakfast bar in the kitchen. I was washing the dishes in the sink when Natalie came up beside me and started rinsing the soapy dishes I had set in the other side of the sink.

"Mom, do you think we could move somewhere far away from here, where no one knows us, after I have the babies?" I stopped washing the dishes and looked up at her.

"Of course, we can. I know this must be hard for you to deal with, especially the kids at school. I can talk to my boss, but we can make this work even if I have to find a new job. I will do whatever I have to, to give you a happy life and leave this one behind us. I was thinking, after you have the babies and have had some time to recover, we should take a nice vacation together, just the two of us, anywhere you want to go!" Natalie had a big smile on her face, the first time I have seen her smile without it being forced or fake in a long time. I gave Natalie a big hug. "I just want you to be happy, sweetheart. I will do whatever it takes!"

The phone rang and I walked across the room with the dish towel in my wet hands, drying them off. "Hello. Yes, this is she. I see. Okay. Thank you for calling."

I hung up the phone and turned to Natalie. "That was the adoption agency. They wanted to let us know that the babies have a home, but unfortunately, they could not keep them together. They will be going to different families, but they are confident this was the best decision since the only family that was willing to adopt twins backed out at the last minute due to a family emergency."

Natalie looked down at the floor, started to cry, and ran out of the room. I could hear the pitter-patter of her footsteps as she ran up the stairs, then across the floor to her bedroom. She slammed her bedroom door closed behind her. I let out a big sigh, pulled out a wooden chair, and sat down. I covered my face with my hands and shook my head, letting out another big sigh as I slouched my shoulders. I needed to give her some space to deal with the news, to get her thoughts together, and she would talk to me when she was ready. I couldn't imagine how hard this was for her to deal with: the raging emotions of a teenager, the hormonal changes of being pregnant by a man that molested and raped her for years, the death of her father, the cruel kids at school, and all the horrible rumors being spread about her. It would be overwhelming enough for a mature adult to deal with all these things, let alone a poor fourteen-year-old girl. I could only hope it was not detrimental to her entire existence and it didn't destroy her emotionally, so she could grow up to be a strong, confident, happy woman. It tore my heart into pieces to see my innocent little girl going through this at such a young age, but I knew I could not drown in despair over things I cannot change. I had to try to make a better life for us moving forward. A nice vacation and moving to a town where no one knows us would be the best options for us to try to move on with our lives and make the best of this awful hand we were dealt in life.

***

Three weeks later, and five weeks before Natalie's due date, I was awakened from a deep sleep by Natalie's screaming. My eyes flew open and my heart sank to the pit of my stomach. I sat up abruptly and swung my legs over the side of the bed until my feet touched the floor while I was searching in the dark with my hands for my glasses on the nightstand next to my bed. After locating them, I pushed them up the bridge of my nose and took off running down the hall to Natalie's bedroom. I found her leaning over the side of her bed, doubled over in pain and holding her very large belly with her small, delicate hands.

"Natalie, what's wrong?" I said in a panic.

"It's the babies! Something's wrong!" Natalie gasped as tears streamed down her rosy cheeks.

"Do you think you can walk to the car? If not, I can call an ambulance and they can carry you out on a stretcher?"

"I think I can walk, Mom."

"You sure? You're going to have to walk down the stairs and I would hate for you to lose your balance and fall."

"Mom, I don't think I can wait until the ambulance gets here. We have to go NOW!"

"Okay, let me help you up." I grabbed both of her hands as Natalie struggled to stand to her feet. We walked hand in hand slowly, her entire body trembling in pain with every step she took. It seemed like an eternity before we made it to the car. I buckled her in and closed the door, then ran to the other side of the car, hopped in and backed out of the driveway as fast as I could. I squealed the tires as I put it in drive and slammed the petal to the floor. It is about a twenty-minute drive to the nearest hospital, but it was 3:00 in the morning and not a single car was on the road. The speed limit was 35mph on this road, but this was an exception and I was driving almost double the legal limit, hoping and praying there were no cops around to pull me over.

The drive took half the time with no traffic and driving like a maniac. We reached the hospital, and I parked in front of the emergency entrance and ran inside to get a wheelchair. A staff in the emergency department grabbed a wheelchair and followed me to the car. Natalie was drenched in sweat and trembling while she held her belly as if she was trying to protect the babies from the pain she was experiencing. The gentleman helped Natalie into the wheelchair and pushed her into the brightly lit hospital and down the hall, then through the emergency room doors where she vanished from sight while I stayed behind, frantically filling out the necessary paperwork.

The babies were born only forty-five minutes after we arrived at the hospital, healthy except for being underweight because they were five weeks early. The boy was born first, at five pounds one ounce, and the girl after, weighing in at four pounds thirteen ounces. Natalie requested that the babies be removed from the room immediately after they were born because she did not want to be tempted to change her mind if she held the babies and got attached. She felt bad for the babies not getting the nurturing from their mother right away, but she knew this was for the best. She was too young, a child herself, to have the responsibility of raising any children. I fear not only that the circumstances of the pregnancy would just be a daily reminder of all that had befallen us, but that we could not be able to give them the love the babies deserved. Their lives would be better in someone else's care, someone who can truly love them for who they are and not how they were conceived. It was unfortunate the babies would be separated, but there was nothing we could do.

"How are you feeling, sweetheart?" I asked with deep concern as I brushed a strand of hair from her eyes.

"Tired and sore. I just want to go to sleep and forget this ever happened." Natalie sighed and turned over on her side, curling into the fetal position with her hands wedged between her thighs.

"Okay, honey. I'll let you sleep. I will be lying in the chair across the room if you need anything." I leaned over and gave her a kiss on the forehead, rubbed her upper arm and whispered in her ear, "I love you. Sleep tight." I walked away and dropped down in the leather recliner across the room and slowly drifted to sleep.

I was awakened by a scream that could have raised the dead, it was dreadful and filled with deep despair. Three nurses came rushing to Natalie's side and pushed her bed through the door in panic, giving me no time to react. I jumped up and rushed out behind them.

"Excuse me!" I yelled. "Where are you taking my daughter? What is going on? What happened to her?" But they were so focused on Natalie I don't think they even heard me. We turned a corner and started down a long, endless hall that seemed to be getting smaller and smaller. I started to breathe heavily, my body felt like I was on fire, and I was getting lightheaded and dizzy. I lost my balance and had to catch myself on a nearby wall to keep from falling. The nurses continued ahead, now picking up their pace. They were almost running as they disappeared through the swinging doors to the emergency room. My eyes were getting heavy and the room seemed to swallow me whole.

The next thing I remember, was being back in Natalie's room feeling groggy and confused. I sat up and took a deep breath, holding my head in my hands. My head was pounding and suddenly felt nauseous. I jumped out of the bed and ran to the bathroom.

What is wrong with me? And where is Natalie?

I got sick and slowly stood to my feet, grabbing hold of the sink to pull myself up. I looked up into the mirror above the sink and the first thing I noticed was how swollen and puffy my eyes were. I was white as a ghost. I just stood there, my hands gripping the edge of the sink to keep me from falling, staring at my reflection in the mirror.

I heard a light knock at the door and then someone opened the door and walked in. "Mrs. Hamlin?" a deep voice echoed through the room.

"I'm in the bathroom, I'll be out in just a minute," I said faintly. "Mrs. Hamlin?" I took a deep breath, got my composure, and turned the doorknob to the bathroom door. "I'm right here," I said as I slowly pushed through the door.

"You shouldn't be out of bed without the help of one of our nurses. You could fall again. You're not strong enough to get up on your own," the doctor said with concern. He was an attractive, tall and slender man with salt and pepper hair and a five o'clock shadow.

"Where is my daughter? What happened to her?" I asked as I slowly walked to the bed and sat down.

"That's why I am here. You fainted and have been resting for several hours. Natalie's body didn't have the stretching capacity required to deliver twins because of her small body frame and young age. She tore her uterus and lost a lot of blood. She was hemorrhaging, and we had to operate immediately to save her life. The good news is that she will be just fine and is recovering now. The bad news is we had to remove her uterus and ovaries because the tear was too severe to repair. She will never be able to have kids again."

I just sat there, distraught, as I tried to absorb all the news. I broke down and cried so hard. it was difficult to breathe.

"Mrs. Hamlin, I know this is not the news you wanted to hear, but I will give you some time to yourself, and Natalie will be brought back in here as soon I check on her again and make sure her vital signs are stable enough to leave the emergency room. If you need absolutely anything, please let us know. We are here to help," he said as he put his hand on top of mine.

His touch was warm and soft. I looked up at him, his eyes were sad. I forced a smile and nodded. He dropped his head and walked out the door, leaving me alone with my thoughts. I started to cry again. I grabbed a tissue from the stand next to the bed and tried to blow my nose, but nothing came out.

How could this be happening to us? Haven't we been through enough? And now this! Natalie is going to be devastated! What can

I say to her to make her feel better? There's nothing! I don't know what to do. I'm at a loss for words. All I can do is be here for her, a shoulder to cry on, someone to listen. My poor Natalie doesn't deserve any of this; she is only fourteen!

Natalie was out of the hospital in five days. She never even glanced in the nursery room when we walked by. I honestly think she was having second thoughts once she found out she would never be able to have children of her own after this operation, but once she signed the adoption paperwork, there was no turning back.

On our drive back to the house, we rode in silence. As I slowly pulled into the driveway, Natalie let out a long sigh. We sat in the driveway for a few moments and Natalie finally spoke. "Mom, I'm ready to start a new life, to forget all this happened, to move on and live somewhere no one knows me. I'm ready to feel normal again and not like an outcast or like a black cloud is hovering over me."

"Let's go inside, honey. I'll make you a BLT for lunch and we can discuss our options and look online for places we would like to move to. It's going to be okay, Natalie. I'm here for you and I'll do whatever it takes to make you happy again!" I said as she wiped the tears running down her cheek. She sniffled and nodded as she pushed the car door open. I grabbed her bag out of the back seat and followed behind as she walked slowly to the front door with her head down.

***

Two weeks later, we pulled out of the driveway, heading for a new life on the beautiful island of Hawaii. As we pulled away, all I could see in my rearview mirror was the For-Sale sign in the front yard of our house. We were leaving behind all our painful memories and hoping to open the doors to a new life where not a soul knew anything about our dark past. We would have the life we always dreamed of, I decided, and my mind was wrapped in nothing but happy thoughts just as a car came speeding through a red light at the intersection, smashing into the passenger's side door where Natalie was seated. All I remember was the shattering of glass and screams echoing through the streets as everything turned black.

Part II

TREVOR

I woke up this morning with a splitting headache. I lay in bed for three hours listening to my parents scream at each other all night. My dad came home late again, and my mom had been drinking all day. To be honest, we hadn't heard from my dad in a few days, and this was happening on a regular basis now.

I'm fifteen and finishing up my sophomore year at Kennedy High School in Butterfield, Virginia. My parents, Travis and Tammy, tried for years to have children of their own, which resulted in their relationship deteriorating. My mother wanted a baby so badly and my father wanted to finish his degree before having any children. My mother gave my father a guilt trip about his commitment to their relationship. He pleaded with her to wait, but she wouldn't have it. She threatened: it's a baby or nothing at all. They loved each other dearly and he didn't want her to leave him, so he sacrificed everything to make her happy. Unfortunately, she didn't get pregnant right away like she had hoped. They went to a specialist, paid an arm and a leg for fertility drugs and the whole nine yards. But what they needed was a miracle. Doctors explained that stress could be causing them problems with getting pregnant. But everything they tried didn't work and my mother was getting very impatient. She was absolutely obsessed. My father was spent and exhausted and started drifting away more and more. He resented my mother, feeling like all she cared about was having a baby. He thought she let the rest of her world crumble around her.

In a last-ditch effort to save their marriage, my father suggested adoption. But even the adoption didn't work. Even though they are still physically married, they are not emotionally—it's more out of convenience now than anything. My mother knows she drove my father away, but instead of talking things out she just drinks to cover up the pain. But it only made things worse; and now, as a result, she has a serious drinking problem. I come home some days from school, and she is passed out on the couch, reeking of booze. She can't keep a job, has stopped cleaning the house, and will go days without showering. My father disappears for days at a time, and my mom thinks he's having an affair, but she doesn't blame him at all. She just looks the other way. She has put on a lot of weight the last few years. I've seen my parents wedding photos and both my parents were a thin, attractive couple. My mom has put on close to a hundred pounds since the wedding and my father looks about the same, except older of course. I think the only reason they stay together is because of me. But I don't even feel like part of this family. My dad is gone all the time and my mom is so drunk she doesn't even know where she is most of the time. I have been taking care of myself since I was twelve. I prepare all the meals, clean the house, do laundry, and somehow am still able to get good grades in all my classes.

I lock myself in my room and lose myself in music. If it wasn't for music, I wouldn't know what to do. It's my way to escape from this nightmare. I really don't hang out with friends much because I'm embarrassed by my mother and don't want people talking. Besides, my mom can't take care of herself. She starts drinking first thing in the morning, and by the time I get home from school, she is beyond drunk and passed out most of the time. I've considered running away, but if I did that, my father would have no reason to stay and my mother couldn't pay the bills without his income and we would lose everything. I could go live with my father, but my mother would have no reason to live at all and probably kill herself from alcohol poisoning. I couldn't live with that either. My mother is a wonderful woman, but she has a problem. I am the typical mamma's boy. My dad worked all the time and would come home late at night, well after I'd gone to bed. It's been only the past three years that he would disappear for days at a time, and that's when my mom started drinking heavily.

It's 7:00 in the morning, and I have to drag my tired ass out of bed and get ready for school with only a couple hours of good sleep to rely on for the rest of the day. I'm surprised I even get out of bed sometimes. I could just stay in bed and sleep. My mother wouldn't know the difference and my father is gone most of the time, so who cares? But my father has always been big on education. If he ever found out I was skipping school or getting bad grades, he would literally kick my ass and take my weekly allowance away. He has a master's degree in business and is the CEO of a small company. He travels for work often, but we used to go on lots of family trips together. I've been to Disney World four times, St. Thomas three times, and Hawaii twice. I've been to the Grand Canyon, Yellowstone National Park and Niagara Falls, just to name a few. We stopped going on family trips about three years ago and my mom thinks that's when my dad began having an affair and taking another woman on those trips instead of us.

My mom says things to me she probably shouldn't when she is drunk, but she is lonely and needs someone to talk to. I've even suggested she go to a therapist to talk to a professional about her problems and get help with her drinking. She always says she will make the phone calls, but she never does. I think she even knows how bad she has gotten, recognizes that she and my father fight about her drinking all the time—when he is home. She yells about how he is gone for days at a time and how she turns to the booze to help with her depression. My dad tries to stay calm as my mother yells at him.

He tells her she wouldn't be so depressed if she got a job, got out of the house once in a while, or hung out with friends. He even suggests that she should lose some weight and take better care of herself. And that he knows that I'm doing most the chores in the house and it shouldn't be my responsibility to take care of the house while he is gone because she's too drunk to do anything. He reminds her that I'm only fifteen and should be studying, doing homework, hanging out with friends, and spending time with a girlfriend. And that I should not be taking care of her drunk ass all the time. You are the mother, he says, and you should be taking care of him, not the other way around.

They fight about the same things all the time and nothing ever changes. I feel helpless. I have learned to put on my headphones and crank the music, so I don't have to hear them fighting anymore.

We live in a nice house with a big yard and an indoor pool. We have a lot of money and I have been spoiled rotten, so I don't complain at all about how our life has become now that our family has been falling apart for the last three years. I help out as much as I possibly can around the house, since my mom is incapable because of her alcoholism. But my dad gives me a $50 allowance every week to do whatever I want with, and he makes sure we are well taken care of. The bills are paid on time, the fridge is always full, and they both have nice cars. I really can't complain because, I tell myself, there are many kids in this world that don't have everything we have and have never been able to take all the trips we have taken. There are a few kids at school who wear clothes two sizes too small for them, look filthy with their hair not cut or brushed well, and walk with their heads down and reek of cigarettes. So I try to remind myself that my life really isn't that bad and could be much, much worse.

I could hear my dad clanging things around in the kitchen. The smell of coffee and breakfast always reminded me that my dad was home. And when he is home, he is a very attentive father. He would make us breakfast in the morning before he had to leave for work and would give me a ride to school. I kicked my legs over the side of the bed and rubbed my eyes as I yawned. I slowly strolled over to my private bathroom, took a quick piss, and headed down the stairs to the kitchen.

"Good morning, Trevor," my dad said, seeming more awake than I was.

"Hi, Dad."

"You ready for some breakfast? I made eggs just the way you like them with bacon and toast."

"I'm starved! Smells great, Dad!" I said with more pep in my step. I walked to the fridge, grabbed the orange juice and poured myself a glass and set it at the table, then walked to the cabinet and grabbed two plates and pulled out the drawer below the black marble countertop that was speckled with glitter. I grabbed two forks and set the table for my dad and me. We both knew my mom wouldn't be up for hours and this was our time to bond in the morning.

My dad walked to the table with the frying pan in his hand and scooped some eggs on my plate, then scooped the remaining on his. He always makes my favorite, scrambled eggs with swiss and cheddar cheese and salsa with a dash of salt and pepper. He then grabbed the plate of bacon on the counter and set it on the table just as two slices of bread popped out of the toaster. He buttered both slices and set one on each of our plates. He then walked over to the coffee pot and topped his mug off and sat down at the table next to me.

"How are things going with you, Trevor?" my dad asked with quiet concern in his tone as he placed his hand on my shoulder.

"I'm okay, Dad," I replied, pushing my eggs around on my plate.

"Are you sure? Your mom has put a lot of responsibility on you. You're just a kid. You shouldn't have to take care of your mother and be responsible for all the household chores when I'm away."

"It's okay, Dad."

"No, it's not! You should be hanging out with friends," my dad replied while taking a sip of coffee. "I have a great idea! I know I'm really hard on you about school, and I'm really proud of you for getting good grades with everything going on with your mom and all, so I was thinking maybe you could skip school just this once and we could go out and do something together, just the two of us?"

My face lit up with excitement. "Absolutely! I would love that!"

We finished eating the rest of our breakfast in silence. My dad stood up while grabbing his dirty plate and coffee mug and walked over to the dishwasher and started loading it with all the dirty pans and dishes from breakfast. I finished gulping the rest of the orange juice. I rinsed off my plate and set my dishes in the dishwasher.

"Hurry up and get dressed and we can head out right away," my dad said while he was bent over loading soap into the tray of the dishwasher. Within just ten minutes we were walking out the front door to the car, on our way to our first destination of the day. My dad handed me the keys as we were walking across the stone walkway leading to our driveway. I have my learners permit and need lots of driving hours, so my dad lets me drive as much as I can when he's home. Our first destination, the arcade.

***

We spent all day having fun, just the two of us, and didn't get home until dark. It was nice since my dad isn't around much. We spent a couple hours at the arcade, then we went out on our boat and sped around the lake for a couple hours enjoying the sun and warm weather. We grabbed a bite to eat at our favorite little burger joint. They have the best fries ever, crispy on the outside, soft in the middle with just the right amount of seasoning—really addicting. After lunch we went on a long scenic drive out of town and talked about everything under the sun. After the drive, went to a movie, and to end the night, we went to dinner at the biggest Chinese buffet around, so many choices it would make your head spin. We just stuffed our faces until we couldn't move anymore.

I think my dad was feeling guilty for not spending much time at home and all the added responsibility on me, having to take care of my drunk mother while he's out of town and all the household chores and keeping up with school. He must have figured I just needed some time to enjoy being a teenager for once and forget about everything else for a day, even school. Which is pretty cool of him, since he's so strict about me getting good grades. He wants me to get into a good college and be successful. As we pulled up to our driveway, I turned off the car and handed my dad the keys.

"Dad, thank you for taking me out all day. I had a great time with you. I hope we get a chance to do it again soon. I feel like I hardly ever see you anymore."

"I know, son, and I'm really sorry for that. I had a really good time too!" he said while the corner of his lip curled up in a half smile. But our fun had ended and we both knew what we were walking into when we walked through that front door. The inevitable.

My dad let out a loud sigh and walked slowly, one foot in front of the other, his head hung low like a beaten man. I just wish we could all be happy again and live a normal life. But who was I kidding? We were a very dysfunctional family, and without my mother getting the help she needed for her alcoholism, this family was doomed. I don't think she even realized the impact her drinking had on this family. She literally drank herself into a coma every day. I would be surprised if she didn't have sclerosis of the liver. My worst fear was to walk home from school one day and find my mother dead. I have had many recurring nightmares of my mother dying. It's not normal but it's reality. My father and I have both begged and pleaded for her to get help, to go to AA or check herself into a treatment program, but she refuses, keeps saying she doesn't have a problem and can stop any time she wants to. I've even gone through the whole house after my mom was passed out on the couch covered in puke one day and raided all the cabinets and other areas I could possibly think of her hiding bottles. And I dumped every single one of them down the drain, full bottles, half-empty ones, others with just a few swallows left in them. That doesn't stop her; she just goes to the store and buys more. She probably thinks she drank all of them too, since she doesn't even know what's going on half the time.

My father paused before unlocking the front door. "Trevor, I just want you to know how bad I feel about not being home much for the last couple years. I know my being gone has put a lot more stress and responsibility on you because of your mother's drinking. And I want you to know I'm going to be home more because it's not fair for you to have to take care of your mom and everything else around here. It's my responsibility, and I've been a coward, hiding from the issue instead of doing something about it. Your mother is in real bad shape, and if she doesn't get help soon, she may drink herself to death. So, I want you to know that I'm not hiding anymore. I'm going to try to fix this family. You don't deserve to live this way. I've been thinking a lot lately, and I think the best option is to put your mom into an inpatient treatment program. I don't know how long she will be in there for, but it will be as long as needed, until she can function again without alcohol. We're talking probably at least six months, maybe longer. It all depends on her progress and when the doctor thinks she is okay to leave. How do you feel about that, son?"

"To be honest, Dad, you must have been reading my mind. Mom's condition is worsening by the day, and I have nightmares of coming home from school and finding her dead. Mom needs help, and I think you should go ahead and do whatever it takes."

My dad patted me on the shoulder. "Just wanted to talk briefly about this before we go inside. I didn't want to ruin our day by talking about your mom the whole time; today was about us having fun together. But I just want you to know your mother most likely won't be home tomorrow when you get home from school. We can visit her in a few weeks, but she needs this time to detox, to reflect and get better."

"Okay, Dad. I think this is what is best for Mom too."

My dad smiled his half-crooked smile and shook his head as he opened the door. My mom was passed out on the couch, her glasses knocked over on the coffee table in front of her. Her drink had spilled and was dripping off the edge onto the floor. My dad and I just looked at each other like we could read each other's minds.

I walked over to my mom, kissed her on the forehead and softly said, "I love you, Mom." I turned away and walked toward my bedroom, knowing that was the last time I would see my mom for a while.

JULIA

I can't believe we are moving again! If I'm not mistaken, we have moved six times and this will make it move number seven. I swear the second I start making friends, we just up and move again. I'm getting to the point that I feel like I shouldn't even try to make new friends anymore because, to my disappointment, my parents will announce we're moving again.

I'm fifteen and will be going into my junior year of high school. I hope this is our last move until I graduate because it would be nice to graduate with people I know instead of complete strangers.

This move in particular has me stricken with anxiety. The idea of a new life, new kids, new teachers and school, makes my stomach do somersaults. Moving makes me feel so alienated and out of place. Sometimes I wish I could magically transform into a turtle and hide in a protective shell that makes me feel comfort and peace. I genuinely hope this move will be different from all the others.

"Julia!" my mom yelled from downstairs, "Have you seen my lotion? I can't find it anywhere."

"Yeah, Mom, I have it. Hold on a minute!" I hollered back.

I walked around all the moving boxes stacked around my bedroom, none quite full just yet but some getting close. I walked into my private bathroom and grabbed my mom's lotion that I had borrowed a few days ago and had forgotten to put back. I absolutely love my mom's lotion. It smells fantastic and leaves my skin feeling amazingly soft.

As I walked down the narrow hallway, I could hear my mom singing faintly to some song playing in her bedroom. To be honest, my mom has a great voice and I don't know why she never pursued a singing career. My mom has been really happy! You can hear it in her voice and see it in her eyes when she talks—they sparkle. She's been singing a lot more and has extra pep in her step lately, mostly due to her promotion, which of course, is the reason we have to make another dreadful move.

But this move may not be so bad after all. My parents told me we're moving into a big house right on a lake. Our backyard opens out to the shore with a private dock and beachfront access. At least that's their selling point to this move. We've moved a lot, just never to a place with a lake right in our backyard, which is pretty sweet. I will definitely enjoy the summer lying on the beach every day, soaking up the sun and working on my tan. But I'm really going to miss the friends I've made here in Olive Hill, Kentucky. It's hard to keep in touch with friends when you move so much. There are a few friends I wrote or sent postcards to keep in touch with after moving, but that usually only lasts for a couple months before I stop hearing from them. Now we are moving to Moneta, Virginia right on Smith Mountain Lake in the Blue Ridge Mountains, which is only 5-1/2 hours away. And my mom will be working in Roanoke as the Origination Banker at

Wells Fargo, which is a huge promotion. But I really hope this is our last move.

What I'll miss most about Olive Hill is the Carter Caves State Resort Park. We would take our camper up there for weekend getaways. We loved to hike, and with more than twenty-six miles of scenic hiking trails, it was the perfect spot. But my favorite was Cascade Cave, created by nature over millions of years and a cool place to explore. It even has multi-cave underground tours.

We also took kayaks out on the water, went on bike rides, and ate at Tierney's Cavern Restaurant. I always ordered either the Chicken Quesadilla or the Kentucky Hot Brown, which is toast points with baked country ham and roasted turkey smothered in cheese sauce, topped with tomato, bacon, cheddar cheese, and baked to perfection.

With Mom's promotion and a big house right on the lake, we may stay in this new location for good. At least, that's what I'm hoping. Mom said there's a mall just a few miles from our new house. What teenage girl doesn't like to shop? It's perfect, so I shouldn't complain much. My parents also mentioned that my best friend Nicole can come stay with us for a few weeks this summer if her parents will let her. So far that sounds promising, at least that's what Nicole said. And since my parents know how much I love Carter Caves State Park, they promised we could come back to visit. This move is definitely starting to sound better and better.

***

The drive to Smith Mountain Lake wasn't too bad. We hit a little traffic, but with the few stops we had to make, we made it to our new house in just a little over seven hours. I didn't know what to expect when we pulled up. Mom and Dad seemed overly excited, but they kept the details pretty much a secret; or as they would put it, the house was "a surprise well worth waiting for." All I knew was that it was big and right on a lake. That was enough for me. We were following behind my dad, who was driving our camper and towing his vehicle behind it. We crept around the neighborhood, slowly admiring the lake and beautiful houses.

The houses here were amazing! I'd only seen houses like this in magazines and in the movies. I just stared out the window in stunned amazement. All the houses on this lake were pristine and very fancy.

Which one is ours? I thought to myself.

"Mom, is this really where we're going to live?"

"Yes, it is!" my mom said with great pride in her voice.

"WOOOOOOW!" I replied in astonishment.

My mom had this huge grin on her face. This was the happiest I think I have ever seen her. I could tell she was ecstatic when she got the promotion at work, and she and Dad went out to celebrate that night. My parents are very much in love. You can tell by the way they look at each other, even after twenty years of marriage. They always make time for date night once a week and have for as long as I can remember; to keep the romance alive.

Now that we are finally here, I think it's really starting to hit my mom. You can see the sparkle in her eyes. My mom is a pretty lady, and I hope I look like her when I am her age. She wears her emotions on her sleeve. You know when she is happy, excited, sad, upset, and angry. There is no second guessing with her, and I respect her for that. She is very honest and so is my dad. I've been raised to believe there is nothing we can't talk about, and how important honesty is.

Then I noticed the moving truck parked on the curb. My dad pulled the camper on the side of the road, got out, walked up to the double iron gates leading to our cobblestone driveway and punched in a few numbers on the keypad. My dad, acting all dramatic, turned around to face us with his hands raised above his head like he was saying, "Ta Da!" as the gates slowly opened to our massive house.

The landscaping leading to the house was astounding, with its perfectly manicured lawn, beautiful array of colorful flowers, and perfectly trimmed bushes wrapping around the house. The porch had massive white pillars on either side with wide French doors leading into the house. I've never seen so many windows, and private balconies led out from each bedroom on the second floor. And above that, which may possibly be the attic, was a huge stained-glass window. The house also had several protruding wings, giving it a unique but picturesque look. There was a huge attached three-bay garage that looked big enough to park even our camper in one stall.

I was ecstatic to see the inside of the house and the backyard leading out to the lake. I just looked over at my mom and it's like she knew exactly what I was thinking. "Want to go check out the inside?" she asked gently, but with just as much excitement in her voice as I felt.

"Absolutely!" I replied, just about jumping out of my skin. I ran up to the front door, but before opening it I turned around to see where my parents were. My dad bent down and picked my mom up off the ground and carried her as she wrapped her arms around his neck. They both were beaming with joy as he walked toward the front door.

The inside of the house was much more beautiful than I could have ever imagined. It was one of those houses people only dream of living in. The foyer ceiling must have been twenty-five feet high with an elegant chandelier made of diamonds hanging from the center of the room. Double staircases led to the second floor on either side, railings wrapping around the entire exposed second floor. Sparkling black quartz tiles covered the floor.

"So, what do you think, Julia?" my dad asked.

Like he even had to ask, I thought.

"Amaaaazing!" I responded with sheer excitement. I just stood there, unable to move from Sudden Shock Syndrome, if that's even a real term, chuckling at my bizarre thoughts.

"Sooooo. Are you going to check out the rest of the house or are you just going to stand there like an idiot?" my dad asked playfully.

"I'm just trying to take this all in, Dad. Give me a break," I replied, while punching my dad playfully in the arm.

"Isn't it stunning?" my mom said, obviously awe stricken.

"Is this a dream?" I cringed after realizing what a dumb question that is.

Both my parents just giggled like little kids.

"More like a dream come true, sweetheart," my mom replied with a big smile, showing her perfectly straight, white teeth.

"I can't believe we actually live here! I can't wait for Nicole to see this place. She is going to freak!" I said, thrilled with over enjoyment.

Where to go first? I thought. *This place is gigantic.*

I turned left and walked through the archway that was made of mahogany, leading into another room. The first thing I noticed was the huge picture window directly in front of me at the end of the room. The window was almost as high as the ceiling, probably twenty feet tall by ten feet wide. There was a stone mantel, electric fireplace with a gigantic TV screen above it that had to be nearly 100 inches, the biggest I had ever seen, which was tucked inside the wall. This wall had openings on either side to get into the next room.

I walked through the left side entry and into the dining area. There were glass sliding doors leading out to a wraparound deck overlooking the lake. A chandelier hung directly above the huge carved mahogany table that dominated the vast space. To the right of the dining area was the kitchen. Directly in the middle of the kitchen was an island with four bar stools. The countertops were made of marble with lots of mahogany cabinets. Above the kitchen sink was a big rectangular window overlooking the lake. All the appliances were stainless steel and the cathedral ceiling above the kitchen was covered completely with massive skylights: a looking glass to the beautiful clear blue sky with hardly a cloud in sight. The windows throughout the house lit up every room with a warm, inviting glow.

I continued to walk through the kitchen to the entryway on the other side. The room was made entirely of windows, what they call a sunroom with a magnificent view of the lake. I pushed through the two wide glass doors that opened to the patio.

A light breeze carried the scent of lilacs and other magnificent flowers; the aromas were intoxicating. The landscaping was pristine. There was an array of colorful flowers, perfectly trimmed shrubs, and a stone walkway that wrapped around the house. The oversized patio had a beautifully sculptured waterfall, an elaborate fire pit and an inground hot tub. There was a gazebo and a rustic oak log swing off to the side of the yard that overlooked the scenic view, which was breathtaking.

At the end of the yard was a big dock that walked out to a boat house. I pinched myself just to make sure this wasn't a dream.

"WOW!"

It just seemed too good to be true. Never in a million years would I have ever imagined we would move into a place like this. All the moving seemed worth it now. I wanted to live here forever. I couldn't wait for Nicole to see our new house. I skipped down to the dock as a thought popped in my head. *I haven't skipped since I was a kid.* I shrugged. *Who cares?* I walked to the end, slipped my sandals off, kicked them to the side, and sat down with my legs dangling over the edge. I dipped my feet into the warm, crystal-blue water and gazed up into the afternoon sky; daydreaming the endless possibilities.

SUMMER VACATION

I was so excited I barely slept last night. I glanced over at the clock hanging on the freshly painted wall in my bedroom. It read, 7:50. Still another four hours before Nicole was supposed to be here. I lay in bed admiring the mint green paint I'd picked out. This shade of green, my favorite, was a lighter shade but not quite pastel. Of course, my dad did most of the work, but I did help a little. A slight smell of paint still lingered in my room, but that's probably because I had to close my window the last couple nights because it had rained.

Last night, while I couldn't sleep, I lay in bed listening to the pitter-patter of raindrops on my window and the echoes of the thunder in the distance while my room lit up like the Fourth of July. I've always loved thunderstorms. Something about them is so peaceful and soothing. The storm was probably the only reason I was able to get any sleep last night. I stretched, let out a big yawn, and walked to a window in my room. I pulled back the curtain and squinted from the bright light that came bursting through my room. The weatherman last night on the news channel said it was going to be mostly sunny with a high around 87 degrees today. *Perfect weather to enjoy the lake*, I thought.

***

The buzzer from the intercom echoed throughout the house. "Nicole!" I was so excited I could barely contain myself. I leapt off the couch in the sunroom, put my book down so as to not lose my place, and ran to the front door to open the gate. I couldn't wait to show her around.

I ran up to the car before they even had time to put it in park. The back-passenger door flew open, and the look on Nicole's face was priceless. "Julia!"

"Oh my!" Mrs. Johnson said in disbelief, as she admired the house. "This is unbelievable!"

"I know," I replied. "Isn't it great? Follow me." I said with a grin from ear to ear. I gave the grand tour of the inside as we made our way to the patio area and the lake out back.

My mom had been preparing appetizers for our guests all morning. My mom really enjoys cooking. You'd think, with the kind of house we live in, we would have a maid and our very own private chef. But my mom takes great pride in her cooking and cleaning. She has to have things done just right. To be honest, I think she has OCD. But I'm not going to complain. Our house is spotless and always smells nice. I didn't like it so much when I was little because my mom always made me pick up after myself. The only room in the house she lets slide even just a little is my bedroom, but I think I may have picked up some of that OCD behavior from her. My bed was always made and my clothes nicely put away. All my clothes were even color coded and all my books organized by alphabetical order and size.

Nicole, on the other hand, was a typical teenager, not very clean or organized at all. She would have piles of clothes all over her bedroom floor. I don't even know if she knew which ones were clean or dirty. But that aside, we got along perfectly. I'm so glad that even though we'd moved, we still lived close enough to visit from time to time. Nicole was to spend three weeks with us this summer because her parents were taking a trip to Hawaii for two weeks.

"Are you hungry, Nicole?" I asked.

"I'm starved!" Nicole replied as she rubbed her belly. We sat down at the patio table while my mom and Mrs. Johnson started bringing out dishes full of all kinds of different finger foods for us to munch on. My favorite was the fresh bread my mom made from scratch, then coated with pesto and layered with baby spinach, tomatoes, and fresh mozzarella cheese melted on top. Nicole and I started shoving food into our faces like we hadn't eaten in days. I don't know why my mom never opened her own restaurant since she loves cooking so much. My dad is a good cook too, but he usually just cooks on the grill. My dad makes a marinade grilled chicken to die for. He won't even tell my mom what his special ingredient is.

After we stuffed our faces to the point we felt like we'd eaten a bowling ball, we decided to take a long walk along the shoreline to work it off. I overheard my dad telling Nicole's parents that the lake is forty miles long, the shore length five hundred miles, and the deepest part is two hundred fifty feet. Just hearing that gave me dreadful thoughts of floating on my back in the middle of the lake with hundreds of feet of water between me and the bottom while sharks swam just below me. It gave me chills just thinking about it.

Nicole and I walked until our toes felt like they were going to fall off, my feet sore and tender with every step I took. We were so busy catching up that we didn't even notice how far we had walked. The air was still, and the sun beat down on us like a fireball blazing in the sky. It was just too hot to tolerate anymore. And all I could keep thinking about was why we left without putting on bathing suits first—that was really stupid. Just then I felt a big shove, lost my balance, and fell into the cool, refreshing lake that lapped against my thirst-hungry skin. I wiped away the droplets that splashed into my face. Nicole was bursting with laughter. Her laughter was quickly replaced by a shriek of surprise when I caught her off guard, grabbed a hold of her ankle, and pulled her into the water next to me. She fell to her hands and knees, and we both erupted with laughter as we lay back and rolled around in the water. Our clothes were soaking wet, but the water rolling over my sunburned skin felt so good.

As I sat up and turned around, I noticed a boy sitting in a chair staring in our direction. Just as our eyes locked, he quickly looked away.

He's pretty cute, I thought. He had short dark hair and a nice tan, but other than that it was hard to tell any other details about him as he was too far away.

I nudged Nicole. "You see that guy sitting over there?" I said quietly, like he could hear what we were saying even though we were far away.

"Yeah, he's cute!" Nicole replied. "You should go talk to him."

"I don't know. I'm pretty shy when it comes to talking to guys. He's probably already got a girlfriend," I said, trying to make an excuse not to go over and talk to him.

"But you never know unless you stop being a chicken shit and get up the nerve to talk to him. What's the worst he could say: sorry, I have a girlfriend? And you'll probably never see the guy again. His family might just be vacationing here, or maybe he lives right next door to you. But you'll never know for sure unless you go talk to him."

"I know, I know," I replied with a slight tone of annoyance. *I wish I was better at this*, I thought to myself. The only way to get over this fear, I knew, was to just start walking toward him. Just then he looked my way again, but this time he held the glance for a few moments longer. There was something about him that was so captivating. I took a deep breath, stood up, and started walking toward him.

I started thinking to myself, "What am I doing? I probably look ridiculous. I'm soaking wet and burned to a crisp." Then a little voice inside me said, "Don't be a coward. You've got this."

The walk seemed so much further than it really was. With every step, I was trying to convince myself to turn around and not make a fool of myself. But I kept walking. The closer I got to him, the more nervous I got. He was much better looking than I'd thought. I gulped. Only a few steps left. I could feel my face turning bright red. It was not like it wasn't already red from being sunburned, but at least my burn might hide me blushing a little.

"Hi, my name is Julia. I just moved here a couple weeks ago from Kentucky. Do you live here too?" I asked, speaking much faster than normal because my nerves were getting the best of me.

"Hi, Julia. It's nice to meet you, I'm Trevor," he replied with a gorgeous smile that made me weak in the knees. "I actually live in Butterfield, just twenty minutes from here.

My dad and I love coming here during the summer. He's at the mechanic's getting our car fixed. I didn't want to sit and wait, so he dropped me off here instead," he said with much more confidence than had been apparent in my voice. "Who's that girl you were rolling around in the water with? Looks like you girls are having fun."

"That's my friend Nicole. She's visiting for three weeks from Kentucky. Her parents are going on vacation, so she is staying with us. We live that way." I turned to my right and pointed to the direction of my house. "I'm just not sure how far from here." I giggled. "We've been walking for a while and our feet our killing us. We didn't plan on walking this far but we were talking and lost track of time."

"My dad texted me a few minutes ago and said he was leaving the mechanic's and would be on his way to come get me. We can give you both a ride back to your place if you would like?"

"Let me go talk to my friend. I'll be right back." I smiled and turned to walk toward Nicole. I couldn't help but smile from ear to ear as I walked toward her.

"Soooooo?" Nicole asked, wanting details of our conversation.

"He offered to give us a ride back to my place. He's just waiting for his dad to come pick him up. Want to ride with them instead of walking all the way back in this heat? My feet are killing me."

"Sure. Anything beats walking right now." Nicole chuckled.

"Okay, I will introduce you to Trevor then."

"Julia and Trevor sitting in a tree...

K * I * S * S * I * N * G," Nicole started reciting.

"Quit it!" I said all flushed as I slapped her in the arm playfully. Nicole just started giggling.

"I think you like him," she said as she raised her eyebrows a couple times.

"Maybe, but cut it out! Please don't embarrass me," I pleaded with Nicole.

"I won't, I promise," she said with a sincere tone, which was reassuring.

We started walking in Trevor's direction, and I noticed an older man standing next to him with a big smile on his face. He gave us a little wave. We both smiled and gave a quick wave back.

As we approached, Trevor's dad spoke up. "Hi. Nice to meet you. I'm Travis, Trevor's dad," he said as he held out his hand for a shake. I held my hand out and noted that Trevor's dad had a firm grip.

I cleared my throat. "I'm Julia," I said shyly, "and this is Nicole."

"Trevor said you two young ladies need a ride back to your house."

"Yes, if you don't mind—our feet are killing us. We're actually not too sure how far it is from here, but we've been walking a long time." I replied.

"Not a problem at all. We are in no hurry. My car is this way," Trevor's dad said as he pointed toward the parking lot. We followed behind him, trying to keep up. As we made it through the crowded parking lot, Travis pressed the remote key as his car lights flashed on and off and unlocked all the doors. We climbed into the back seat of the roomy black SUV that smelled of leather and cologne. "So which direction, ladies?" Trevor's dad spoke up as he slid his sunglasses up the brim of his nose.

"Take a left here," I said, focusing on the road. We drove in silence as I was searching the massive houses around the lake, trying to find mine. After driving for ten minutes, I spotted it. "We're right here." I pointed at the beautiful house we were approaching.

"You live here?" Trevor said, shocked.

"Yep!" I said proudly.

"Wooooow."

I just smiled. "You want a tour?" I asked all giddy.

"Can we, Dad?" Trevor asked with excitement.

"Only if you think your parents would be okay with it."

"Yeah, I'm sure they will be. They really want me to make new friends out here."

I gave them the grand tour. Afterward, my mom invited Trevor and Travis to stay for dinner. My dad grilled burgers and hot dogs while my mom made pasta salad and potato salad in the kitchen.

Everyone sat outside enjoying each other's company on our spacious patio. The dads drank beer and the moms drank wine, while we teenagers had freshly squeezed lemonade.

After we finished up with dinner, Nicole and I decided to finally slip on some bathing suits and go for a nice swim. Trevor, of course, joined us. The water felt refreshing after the day we'd had in the heat. We splashed around until the sun went down and the moon danced across the water. The soft glow of the moon made the water sparkle like tiny diamonds. A motion censored spotlight from the boathouse turned on at dusk. It was starting to get dark and my father was hollering at us from the patio to come in.

"I guess we better get out guys," I said as I swam to the shore.

"My dad's probably going to want to take off as soon as we go inside," Trevor replied.

"Maybe you can hang out again with us tomorrow," Nicole, the last one out of the water, said.

"I'll have to see if my dad will drive me, but that would be fun." Trevor turned and looked at me with a slightly longer stare. I grinned and looked away shyly. There was something about Trevor that drew me to him. I couldn't quite put my finger on what it was, but I think I might grow to really like him.

A
CRUSH

The next three weeks flew by. Before I knew it, Nicole's parents were back from their vacation and they were heading back home to Kentucky. And that's when it hit me. Summer vacation was ending soon, and I'll be the new kid in school—again. Something I wasn't looking forward to. A new school, new faces, new teachers—just a bunch of strangers and new places I would have to get used to. I used to be a social butterfly, but the more I moved the less fun meeting new people had become. You would think being forced into these situations would make me a pro at making new friends, but it was doing the complete opposite. Making new friends can be exhausting, especially when you know it's just for a short period of time.

The last three weeks Trevor had spent three days a week with Nicole and me. I think Nicole felt a little like a third wheel when we all hung out together, but she was happy that I had met a nice guy out here in Virginia. Trevor and I hadn't made it official yet, but things were definitely going in that direction.

He is a Cancer and I am a Scorpio. I've always been fascinated with astrology. Our signs say—we are a perfect match for each other, being that we are both water signs, but we are also, two emotionally intense signs. It also states that we have a great deal in common, and much potential to keep a relationship passionate and strong, which is promising. The only problem is, we are both too shy to make the next move. But I see the way he looks at me, and I think he knows I like him as more than just a friend. We just haven't had a chance to hang out alone yet, and I'm quite nervous about it. Nicole is a lot better at this kind of thing, you know, the boy thing. She's a natural. I clam up and am a loss for words when I really like someone. She helped fill in those awkward silences and make things less weird. So, now with her being gone, I didn't know how things were going to go with Trevor. I hope I don't make a fool of myself.

Mom and Dad really seem to like him too. I think my dad and Trevor's dad are really hitting it off too. Mr. Williams always hangs out and has a couple beers with my dad when he comes to pick up Trevor. I still haven't met Trevor's mom. In fact, he is pretty quiet about her. All I know so far is that she is away, and he isn't sure when she will be back. He gets upset whenever she is brought up in conversation, so I don't push the issue. When he is ready, he will tell me. We only met three weeks ago.

Our first time alone together will be this weekend. I'm going to his house for the first time. He has been coming here every time we hang out, probably because Nicole was staying with me and we live on the lake and have more to do here. I'm excited go to his place. I haven't left my house or the lake since we moved here except once to check out the mall with my mom and Nicole. I picked up a few new outfits for the new school year and we grabbed some lunch at a nice restaurant in the city. As much as I loved my new house and living on a lake, I needed some new scenery. I haven't been to Butterfield or any other towns or cities in Virginia, and so, I thought, going to Trevor's would be a nice change.

On days Trevor and I aren't hanging out he will shoot me a text a couple times a day to see how my day is going and what I'm up to. We would probably hang out more except he works four days a week at Taco Bell in Butterfield. I love all kinds of Mexican food, but I haven't been to a Taco Bell in over a year; and once he mentioned he worked there, I've been craving it ever since. So I convinced Mom and Dad to take me up there for lunch today.

***

I slept in late and need to shower quick before we head out for lunch. I walk across my soft rug that tickles my bare feet every time I touch it, wondering for the millionth time what the rug is made of. It is the softest rug I've ever felt, and even though I've had it for years, I've never figured out what it's made of. It's just a shade darker than the mint green walls I painted my room. My bedroom floor is covered in mahogany which is shiny and always sparkling clean.

Since my parents hired a maid to keep the house spotless, everything is especially clean. She sweeps and mops all the floors and dusts and polishes all the woodwork. She puts fresh linens on our beds every day, washes and folds our laundry, and cleans all our dishes. Bathrooms are always clean and smell nice with fresh clean towels. Maria does an amazing job, but my parents probably pay her good money to keep the house looking the way it does. She lives in our guest house. She minds her business and is very friendly, but she is quiet and keeps to herself. Mom said she is a widow, says her husband passed away years ago and she is lonely. The bank took her house, cars, and everything she owns because she couldn't afford them. She stayed at home and cooked and cleaned while her husband worked and never had a job a day in her life outside of the home.

Her four children are all grown and have kids of their own. They come and visit her from time to time, but the guest house is big enough to house her and all her children and grandchildren comfortably. My parents have invited her to eat dinner with us a few times, but she always says that she doesn't want to seem rude, but she would rather eat alone. I think she refuses the invitation because she doesn't want to intrude on our family time; she seems very old fashioned like that. I feel very sad for Maria. She always has a smile on her face every time I see her, but there is definite sadness behind her eyes.

I was downstairs and ready by noon. I walked into the kitchen to grab a glass of orange juice. My parents were sitting at the island across from each other, holding hands and talking, two lovebirds who just can't get enough of each other. You can tell how madly in love they are just by the way they look at each other.

"You all ready to go?" my dad said as he glanced over at me pouring a glass of juice.

"Yep. I've been ready for hours," I said with a smirk.

"Oh yeah, I'm sure you have," my dad said sarcastically. My mom just chuckled. "Let's go then," my dad said as he stood up and held out his hand to my mom. They walked hand in hand to the front door while I gulped down my orange juice, then walked over to the sink and rinsed out my glass.

The ride to Taco Bell seemed much longer than twenty minutes, probably because all I'd had was a glass of orange juice since 6:00 last night. I could feel my stomach rumbling—it wasn't very happy with me. Trevor was working today. I had a text from him when I woke up at 10:30.

We had to park at the far end of the lot and walk for what seemed like a mile. The line inside was long and cars wrapped around the drive-through. Trevor had mentioned it was busy here, but I never thought it would be this busy.

There were about nine people in front of us in line, and almost every table was full. I tried standing on my tippy toes to see if I could see Trevor working, but there were just too many people in the way.

"Do you know what you want, Julia? You'll have to grab us a seat or we may not have anywhere to sit," my dad said as he looked around impatiently.

"Just order me a combo #5 with soft tacos and a side of guacamole," I said loud enough to speak over the crowd. "I'll grab us some sauce packets, napkins and straws." I walked over to the station next to the fountain machine and caught a glimpse of Trevor. I waved but I don't think he saw me. I grabbed the only table open, which was right next to the window. It took Mom and Dad a while to order. They finally walked over and sat down. Mom handed me a cup. There were only a couple people left in line now and a few tables were opening up. I saw Trevor, and he looked up at that moment with a big grin on his face and waved. I waved back. I filled my cup with Dr. Pepper and walked back over to the table my mom and dad were sitting at. They still hadn't called our name yet.

A few minutes later Trevor came walking over with our tray of food. "Hey, Julia, Mr. and Mrs. Hendricks!"

"Hi, Trevor," we all said in unison. I just giggled.

"Wow you were right when you said you were busy here," I said, then took a gulp of my soda.

"Yeah, but it just gets like this during peak hours. It will slow down in a little bit. My manager said I can take a break since you guys are here, and so I'm going to whip up something quick to eat if you don't mind if I join you."

"Not at all, Trevor. Glad you can come eat with us," my mom said while she was unwrapping her taco.

He dashed behind the counter. I had already scarfed down the two tacos before Trevor came back with his food—I was hungry. I quickly grabbed a napkin when I saw Trevor heading to our table and wiped my mouth, hoping he hadn't just seen me inhale my food. I probably looked like a garbage disposal. Trevor sat down next to me, and I felt my heart flutter and I clammed up, a million thoughts rushing into my mind but nothing making it to my lips. I got so nervous around him that I just stared with a blank face. I know Trevor must have thought I'm weird or that I don't like him, but that's far from the truth.

"Hey, Julia," he said with a smirk, "how's the food?" I raised my fingers to my lips to hide the bite I had just taken. "Good... I was starving!" I giggled.

"So am I," Trevor said. "You want to know the hardest part about working here?"

"What's that?" my dad replied.

"Being surrounded by food when you're hungry and watching everyone else eat." Trevor laughed.

"I can imagine," my mom responded as she cleared her throat. We visited with Trevor for another twenty minutes but had to let him get back to work.

On the ride back home, all I could think about was Trevor: his beautiful green eyes, tan skin, and amazing smile with the most perfectly straight white teeth. That sparkle in his eyes was so mesmerizing. I couldn't wait to spend time with him alone on the weekend. I was not sure how awkward or nervous I would be, but I was looking forward to it.

While I was gazing out the car window, I noticed how dark the sky was becoming. It looked like we were driving right into a storm. I could see lightning flashing in the distance and the wind was starting to pick up, and then the downpour started. It was hard to see anything in front of us, even with the wipers on full speed. My dad had to slow way down and pull over on the side of the road.

"I guess we'll sit here and let this storm pass through. There's no way I'm driving in this mess. I can't see a thing!" my dad said, obviously frustrated.

I stared as the rain pounded on the windows, causing a blanket of distorted images. I usually love the sound of rain because it always seems to relax my busy mind, but this rain was disturbing. The next thing I knew my body was thrashed around violently, the seatbelt cutting into my skin, and my face smashed into the back of the passenger's seat. All I could hear was horrific screams and glass shattering all around me as I got swallowed into a black, empty hole.

A
BAD
FEELING

I was glad that Julia and her parents came to visit me. It was a stressful day at work, but the second I saw Julia standing in line, all my anxiety disappeared. She had that effect on me. She was shy but in a cute kind of way, and I liked that about her. There are plenty of snotty girls in high school who think they are better than everyone else.

I doubted Julia realized how naturally beautiful she really is. She doesn't wear any makeup, and girls her age tend to go overboard with makeup and look so fake. I caught myself daydreaming about Julia a lot. She did this thing with her hair, and I also doubted she knew she was doing it, but she twirled it around her finger a lot. It must be a nervous quirk. Now that Nicole was back home, I could spend some alone time with Julia and hoped that something more happened with our friendship. I really liked her, and I thought she might like me too; but it was hard to say because she was so quiet at times. It was hard to read her. All I knew was she was constantly on my mind. I would text her more, but I was afraid I might annoy her.

I was pretty nervous about this weekend. Julia had never been to my house before. We were always at hers since she lived right on the lake and there was a lot more to do at her house. I wracked my brain every night as I lay down for bed, thinking about what we should do. I didn't want to bore her. I wanted to do something fun and exciting. I thought maybe we could go to the arcade and play games, but that's more of a guy thing and I wasn't sure if she would enjoy that. Then I was thinking of taking her to the aquarium, or maybe to this new zip line that just opened about half hour from here, or maybe the fair. Or maybe just something simple, like dinner and a movie. But I didn't want it to seem cliché or too much like a date. I wanted her to feel comfortable, like we were just having fun hanging out as friends. For all I knew, she only wanted to be friends, but something told me deep down inside that she wanted more; but I also knew that I could be wrong.

All this over-thinking was making my head spin. Maybe this was what having a crush feels like. I'd never really been interested in any girl before. Maybe because I'd been taking care of my mom all these years and had all these extra responsibilities most kids my age don't have to worry about. I didn't have time to think about girls. Besides, I would have been too embarrassed to take them home. They'd take one look at my mom and run for the hills.

But now that she was away getting the help she needed for her alcoholism, I didn't have to worry as much anymore. She had been in treatment for six weeks now.

The doctor kept my dad up-to-date on her progress. Most inpatient rehab centers recommend no visitors for the first three to six weeks depending on their progress and the severity of the disease. In fact, I never knew drinking too much was considered a disease. My mom's doctor, Dr. Harrington, said it would be best for her to not have any visitors for the full six weeks because she was having a difficult time coping with the severe withdrawal.

Since I had plans to hang out with Julia on Saturday, my dad was thinking of us going to visit Mom on Sunday and making a day of it because she was four hours away at one of the best treatment centers in the country. He said I could pick the restaurant we stopped at for dinner on our way home Sunday night. A nice hole-in-the-wall burger or steak place sounded pretty good, or maybe we would pass a Golden Corral on our way home.

A couple loud claps of thunder startled me, snapping me back into reality. My mind seemed to wander quite a bit at work. I didn't have much longer before my shift was over for the day. The light flickered and the rain was pounding hard now, ricocheting off the road. I could hear sirens off in the distance; quite a few of them, actually. They were getting louder as they approached, emergency vehicles zipping past us on the main street. Drivers got out of the way as the emergency vehicles blew through the stop lights. They were in a big hurry to get somewhere. Must have been a bad accident. I hoped Julia and her parents made it back home safely.

I grabbed my phone out of my back pocket, then hesitated. They literally just left not long ago, maybe twenty minutes or so. I don't want to seem desperate by texting her too soon, and so I thought maybe I'd wait a while. I slipped the phone back into my pocket. I glanced up at the clock, 1:25. My shift would end in thirty-five minutes. A sudden dreadful feeling hit me like a massive tidal wave. I felt sick to my stomach and a horrible sharp pain ripped through my head like I had been hit with a hammer. Something wasn't right!

Weird things like this have happened to me in the past. I'm not sure what was causing it, but I felt like I just got hit by a train, my skin felt like it was on fire, and my head felt like it is going to explode. The room started spinning, faster and faster and I felt like I was going to pass out. I needed to sit down. Then, just as quickly as it came on, it all just vanished into thin air. I had been to the doctor after an incident like this occurred before, but my test results came back normal. The doctor claimed that I'm perfectly healthy. But something that felt so unquestionably intense and extreme certainly couldn't be healthy or normal. Then the whole set of symptoms just vanishing into the unknown dynamics of my subconscious without a single physical side effect or explanation is was just plain weird, if you ask me.

I finished the rest of my shift and clocked out. The rain was just a light drizzle now, but the parking lot was covered in puddles. The air smelled of fresh rain and a double rainbow had formed in the sky, rays of sunlight escaping through the clouds, leaving a shimmering glow in the reflection of the puddles. I have always loved how it smells after a thunderstorm, refreshing and delightful, as if the world had been washed clean.

My dad was waiting in the parking lot. I slipped into the car with drenched shoes as my dad turned the car engine over.

"How was work?" my dad asked.

"Busy, but Julia and her parents stopped in for lunch today." I pulled out my phone and texted Julia: *Thanks for visiting me at work today, it was a nice surprise :) Hope you made it home safely after the storm that passed through town earlier. Can't wait to see you this weekend.*

I reached over and turned the radio on. "Believer" by Imagine Dragons was playing. I cranked up the music. Drowning myself in good music always put me in a good mood, but I just couldn't seem to shake the horrible, daunting feeling that came on out of nowhere earlier. I decided I wasn't going to worry about it too much, as mysterious and confusing as it was. I wasn't going to let it ruin my day or freak out my dad.

As we pulled into the driveway at home I glanced at my phone. Julia still hadn't responded to the text I sent her. That's not like her. I usually got a text back by now. I assumed she must be busy and wondered what she was up to. My dad had to rush back to work; he picked me up during his lunch break on days I was scheduled to work. I thought maybe I'd swing by the arcade and play a few games. I unlocked the garage door as my dad backed out of the driveway. He honked the horn and I turned around and waved. I reached around the corner and flipped on the light switch in the garage, walked over and grabbed my bike, which was hanging on the wall, and started my two-mile ride to the arcade.

It will be nice next year when I get my license and can drive everywhere instead of relying on my mom or dad to take me places. I'd been getting some behind-the-wheel practice with my dad a little bit this summer, trying to rack up some driving hours with this learner's permit. I'd also been saving the money I earned at my summer job to buy a car. I wasn't sure what I wanted to get yet, but Dad had been talking about taking me car shopping in the next couple of months once I had enough saved for a down payment.

I played at the arcade for over two hours. Time flew when I played games, wrapping my mind into a whole different world of dimensions: racing cars, fighting zombies, attacking aliens or monsters. It let me escape the real world momentarily, but it was also addicting, and I could spend all day wrapped up in this fantasy world. The arcade also had a small snack bar with pizza by the slice, hot dogs, nachos, pretzels, popcorn, and a variety of candy bars and plenty of different drinks. So, you could literally stay here all day since you didn't have to leave when you got hungry. And attached to the building was a movie theater. If you walked down the north hallway, you walked right into it. A couple of the rooms played 3D movies, which was really cool to watch but I hadn't seen anything playing recently that I wanted to see. Maybe one day I would take Julia to watch a 3D movie with me.

That thought reminded me that I still had not heard back from Julia since she left Taco Bell. I glanced at my phone again—nothing. Now I really started to worry. It had been about three hours since I sent the text after work. I looked up at the clock hanging on the back wall: 5:15. Dad would be back at the house a little before 6:00, and so I stepped outside, grabbed my bike, and took the scenic way back home because there would be less traffic at this time of day.

Shortly after I got home, my dad came walking in with a couple of bags. The aromas were seeping through and bursting into the air. "I hope you're hungry for some Chinese?" my dad said as he set the bags on the counter in the kitchen. "I grabbed us the sesame chicken you like so much, with some fried rice, egg rolls, and spicy Szechuan green beans." He pulled the containers out of the paper bags and set them out for us to dish from.

"I'm starved!" I replied. I piled the food on my plate. I know I'll regret it later, but I hadn't eaten Chinese in so long and planned to stuff my face until my stomach exploded. I started shoveling food the second I sat down at the dinner table.

"Looks like someone was hungry!" my dad said with a smirk.

"You have no idea!" I said, shoveling more forkfuls of fried rice into my mouth. "Thanks for dinner, Dad. You must have read my mind."

"You bet!" he said with a big smile. It had been nice spending more time with my dad after so many years without seeing much of him. I really didn't blame him. My mom was a disaster, wallowing in depression and self-pity. I didn't even want to be around her. She reeked of booze all the time and smelled of B.O. because she'd go days without showering. Alcohol destroyed her and this family, and I really hoped this treatment helped her recover and we could start repairing the broken pieces left in its destructive path.

I was in fact looking forward to seeing my mom on Sunday, but at the same time, it was nice not having to take care of her and finally getting to spend quality time with my dad. He really was a broken man. I knew he loved us, and he was a good father, but I also knew he had been unfaithful to their marriage. Since my mom is trying to get the help she needed to get better, he will have to try to gain her trust again. I hope this means that my dad will be around a lot more now.

I turned the TV on in the living room, sat down on the couch, and kicked my feet up on the coffee table. I grabbed my phone out of my pocket. Julia still hadn't texted me since she left Taco Bell. Seven hours now with no word from her. Maybe it's nothing, I told myself. She may have lost her phone or dropped it in a puddle after the storm.

I started texting: *Hi, Julia. I hope you're having a great day. It was nice seeing you today* :)

My dad came in and sat down in his recliner. "What's bothering you, Trevor? You looked perplexed," my dad said with concern.

"Oh, I just haven't heard from Julia since she and her parents came to visit me at work for lunch today, which was seven hours ago now." I shifted uncomfortably. "She usually texts me back shortly after I shoot her a text. I haven't heard a word from her, and I've sent two texts now."

"I wouldn't worry about it too much. I'm sure it's nothing, son. She just might be busy."

"I know but they were driving back home when the bad storm came through town, and not too long after that a bunch of emergency vehicles came flying through the stop lights with their sirens blaring, most likely hurrying to an accident."

"How about this? If you're that worried, and you don't hear back from her in the morning, I'll go into work late tomorrow and we can swing by her house to give you some peace of mind."

"You'd do that for me?" I replied, surprised.

"Yeah, of course I will. I can tell you really like her, and you'll worry yourself to death while I'm at work all day. I'm sure she's fine, but—"

"Thanks, Dad!" I interrupted.

"Let's find something funny to watch. It'll be a nice distraction," My dad said while he scrolled through the guide. "I'd suggest making some popcorn, but I think we're both too full for popcorn after that Chinese food we just devoured," my dad said with a chuckle.

"Yeah, you're right, way too stuffed!"

E. A. Owen

THE
TRAGEDY

I woke up at 6:56 in the morning, and the first thing I did was check my phone—nothing. *Good Morning Sunshine* :) I texted, half asleep. I could smell the coffee, which meant my dad was up. I jumped in the shower quickly, knowing we were going to have to rush out the door soon so my dad wouldn't be too late for work. I hurried as fast as I could to get ready.

My dad was sitting at the kitchen table, enjoying his coffee and reading the paper. "Good Morning!" my dad said as he set the newspaper on the table and took a sip of coffee. He was a morning person, but me, I need a couple hours before I'm fully awake and alert. "Any word from Julia?"

"Noooo," I said, disappointed.

"If we go over there this early in the morning, do you think she will be awake?" my dad asked.

"Probably not. She usually sleeps late, but I'm sure one of her parents will be awake by the time we get there."

"Let's get going then," my dad said, taking his last sip of coffee, then setting his mug in the sink.

It was only a twenty-minute drive, but it sure seemed to take closer to an hour. I just sat quietly, gazing out the window at all the clouds in the sky. We finally pulled up to the gate in front of her house and I pushed the buzzer, hoping that someone would answer. But there was nothing but silence. *Maybe they were still sleeping*, I thought, but I doubted her parents would still be sleeping.

An older lady was pulling weeds in the yard next door. I walked over to her. "Excuse me," I called. The lady stood up and turned around.

"Can I help you?" she said in a gentle voice.

"Yes. My friend Julia lives in that house over there," I said as I pointed. "Oh yes, what a sweet family they are. I think the girl's name is Jessica?"

"Julia," I corrected her.

"Why, that's right."

"By chance did you see any of them around here yesterday?" I asked.

"Now that I think of it, I saw them leave yesterday around lunchtime but haven't seen anyone around since."

"Okay, thank you, ma'am."

"No problem," she replied and went back to weeding. I walked back to my dad, who must have tried buzzing them at the gate while I was talking with their neighbor.

"Still nothing," my dad said. "What did you find out from the neighbor?"

"She saw them leave around lunchtime but hasn't seen them since," I replied, the worry apparent in my voice.

"But they have quite a bit of privacy, with the gate, trees and bushes bordering their property. Maybe they came back while she was inside," my dad implied.

"But that doesn't explain why I haven't heard from Julia and why no one is buzzing us in."

"Maybe they're still sleeping," my dad suggests, he trying to be more positive while I was thinking the worst.

"What if something did happen? What if they got into a car accident on their way home yesterday? How would we even find out?" I had a million thoughts screaming in my head. I could feel the anxiety boiling inside me.

"I can make a few phones calls on the way back to our house to see if I can find anything out. I have a friend who is an EMT in town, and maybe he knows who was involved in the emergency call yesterday during the storm," my dad said as he climbed back into the car.

He dialed his phone. "Hi, Alex. It's Travis. I'm doing good, and how are you? Actually, I was calling because my son is worried his friend may have been involved in a car accident on their way home yesterday afternoon during the storm we had, and I thought maybe you had some information. Trevor told me that several emergency vehicles were rushing somewhere shortly after his friend and her parents left his work. Do you have any idea what happened yesterday?" My dad paused for a while, listening to his friend. I couldn't make out anything that was being said, just some mumbling on the other end of the phone.

"Are you sure? Okay, and thanks for your help Alex. Talk to you soon. Bye." I could tell something was wrong and my dad must have been searching for the words to tell me.

"What did he say, Dad? Does he know anything about the accident yesterday and who was involved?" I aksed impatiently, expecting the worst but crossing my fingers it wasn't Julia and she was okay. It took a while for my dad to compose himself.

"I think it's best I drop you off at home, then swing by the hospital to get some more detailed information about the people involved in the car accident yesterday."

"No! I want to come with you," I demanded. "Do you think it may have been them?" I asked as my stomach did somersaults.

"He's not sure who was involved. He just said that it was bad! Two vehicles were involved. One car had three people in it, two adults and a teenager, and the other had two adults. Everyone involved was rushed to the hospital with serious injuries. He didn't have any names or much detail about the accident. But he did say they are all at Eastside General Medical Center," my dad said nervously.

"I'm coming with you. I need to know if Julia is there!" I said a little choked up. I felt like a golf ball was lodged in my throat and I was having a hard time talking. I had a bad feeling about this.

We drove the rest of the way to the hospital in silence. We pulled into the visitors' parking lot and my dad found a parking space quite a way from the entrance. The hospital seemed overly busy today. Not that I come here often, but I wouldn't think it was this busy all the time. As we walked toward the hospital, my dad pulled out his phone and made a call.

"Hi, Matt; it's Travis. I was just calling to let you know I won't be coming in today. An emergency has come up. I'll keep in touch." We stopped at a crosswalk and waited for the lights to turn, then proceeded to cross the busy road, walked through automatic revolving doors into the hospital, and approached the front desk.

"Hi, my name is Travis. My friend who works as an EMT let us know about a two-car collision that happened yesterday afternoon involving five people. All of them were all rushed here with serious injuries. I was wondering if you could tell me if any of those patients involved may have been the Hendricks? The girl's name is Julia, and her parents' names are Alex and Janessa."

The girl behind the counter, who couldn't have been more than twenty, just froze and turned white as a ghost. Her eyes saddened and she was trying to choke out words, but no sound came out. She paused and looked down, trying to compose herself. I could sense that the news she was about to give us was going to be hard to hear.

"Sir, I'm so sorry to tell you this…but Alex and Janessa…were pronounced dead at the scene, and their daughter Julia…is in a medically-induced coma."

Tears started streaming down her cheeks, but she wiped them away quickly. My dad just stood there in shock. He didn't say a word.

I could feel a hard ball forming in the back of my throat. "This can't be happening. It must be a mistake. I just saw them yesterday afternoon."

That's when it hit me. I was the last person to see them alive. The temperature in my body was climbing fast, my hands started trembling, and a cold sweat was forming at the edge of my forehead and the back of my neck. The room started to spin, and I felt like I was going to get sick. My knees started to give out from under me. I was being swallowed into complete darkness.

KENTUCKY

I visited Julia in the hospital every day for the next week. She was nonresponsive but alive. The doctor had her in a drug-induced coma due to her head injury and brain swelling. It was very difficult seeing her this way.

When my dad wasn't working, he did some private investigation of his own, trying to find a relative or friend of Julia's to let them know what happened. I suggested going to the town she had moved here from and knocking on every door until we found Nicole and her parents because I never did catch a last name while she was visiting. I should have asked more questions or paid closer attention. But I never thought in a million years that this would have happened. The only things I knew about Nicole was she lived in Olive Hill, Kentucky, was friends with Julia and the same age, and her parents took a trip to Hawaii for a couple weeks while she stayed with Julia. No last name, birthday or school she attended.

Our only advantage was that Olive Hill was a small town with a population of fifteen hundred people. Although the local police had been no help, we might only have to ask a few people where Nicole lived before finding someone who knew her. But since Julia had moved so much, I'm not even sure if contacting Nicole would be of any help. I don't even know if Nicole, let alone her parents, knew much about Julia's family. But my dad was determined to find Julia's family so that Mr. and Mrs. Hendricks could have a proper burial.

***

"Wake up, Trevor! We're going to Kentucky," my dad said in a hurry. He flipped on my bedroom light and I pulled the blanket over my head.

"Right now?" I said half asleep. "Yep! Got the car all packed up. We're going to find Nicole and her parents. I haven't been able to sleep for a week. I just toss and turn, thinking about how no one knows what has happened to Julia and that her parents are both…in a better place."

I noted that my dad can't bring himself to say that they are dead. It sounded awful, but there was no other way to put it. But I don't like saying it either. "Can I at least jump in the shower quick before we leave?"

"Only if you make it quick, and I mean like five minutes quick," my dad replied like he had already drunk an entire pot of coffee, which he probably had. I climbed out of bed and stretched my arms outward while I let out a deep yawn. I looked over at my dad, who was pacing back and forth like a maniac. I just shook my head as I walked to my bathroom and closed the door behind me.

Five minutes later I was showered and dressed. At least my dad wasn't pacing back and forth in my room anymore. "Hurry up, Trevor. I don't have all day!" he yelled from the other room. He must have heard the bathroom door open, but how? It didn't even creak. I'd never be able to sneak out the house if I wanted to, given that man's amazing hearing. My dad should have been some secret undercover spy or detective. No one could hide from him with his ultra-sensitive hearing, which seemed like that of a moth. I learned in Biology 101 that moths have the capability of hearing sound frequencies of up to 300kHz, blowing away our human abilities of about 20kHz. Who knew the moth had a superhero gene? Researchers suspect that the moth's extraordinary sense of hearing is used to outwit its main predator, the bat. I think I'm going to start calling my dad the Moth Ninja. I chuckled at the thought. My dad was close to getting a black belt in karate when he was a kid. It takes a lot of dedication to become a black belt. I'm pretty sure my dad has a brown belt, which comes after white, yellow, gold, orange, green, blue, and purple belts; which is very impressive.

I've noticed my mind wandering more lately, and I gave myself a hard time for having such ludicrous thoughts now, at a time like this. I grabbed my backpack out of my closet and stuffed a bunch of clothes into it, not knowing how many days we would be gone.

"Trevor let's go! I'm going stir crazy in here," my dad hollered from the kitchen.

"Give me a second; I'm grabbing a few things," I responded with an annoyed tone. I grabbed the book from my nightstand that I had been reading at night to help me fall asleep and distract me from worrying about Julia so much. And of course, I couldn't forget my baseball cap, which was sitting on my dresser. I took a quick look around my room to see if anything caught my eye before heading out the door. But of course, you always have that overwhelming feeling like you're forgetting something before a big trip. Not like I had much time to prepare for this trip anyway since I literally found out about it eight minutes ago.

As I walked out my bedroom door, I swung my backpack around my shoulder and slipped my hat on while I thought, "Kentucky, here we come."

My dad was tapping his foot by the front door and let out a big sigh. "Finally!" he said with frustration.

I just shook my head and walked outside without saying a word. The sun was just coming up over the mountains, and a cool breeze tickled the back of my neck and sent chills down my body. I turned around as my dad was just locking the door. "Dad, I need to grab a hoodie quick before we leave." My dad just gave me that look, like I better hurry, or he was going to lose it. I grabbed the first hoodie I could find hanging in the closet behind the front door and yanked it off the hanger, which fell to the floor with a clang. I just kicked it to the back and slammed the door shut, then took off to the car, threw my backpack in the back seat, and climbed into the passenger seat. My dad was in the driver's seat just seconds later.

It was a long drive to Kentucky, five and a half hours, and Dad and I took turns picking songs on the radio but didn't say much. It was a relaxing drive. I just gazed out the window enjoying the view. I love the outdoors and traveling to new places. I had never been to Kentucky before, and neither had Dad. I broke the silence.

"Have you thought much about how we are going to find Nicole and her parents?"

"I figured, since Olive Hill is a small town, it shouldn't be too hard. Just stop at a few businesses and ask if they know them. If I remember correctly, his name is James and his wife is Katherine, and of course there's Nicole." My dad has always been great with names, which is a good thing because without names it was hopeless. We only met them that one time at Julia's house that first day. I just shrugged. It was worth a try. We might get lucky.

***

When we finally made it to Olive Hill, Kentucky we stopped at a small diner on the edge of town to grab a bite to eat before starting our investigation. The place was small, with just a few booths and tables. There was a young, pretty girl with long, golden blonde hair standing behind the counter. She looked up and smiled when we walked in. We seated ourselves at a booth in the corner by a window. The girl walked over to our table with two glasses of water, pulled straws out from her apron and set them on the table in front of us.

"Good afternoon! How are you fine gentleman doing on this beautiful day?" the waitress asked cheerfully.

"We're just fine. How about yourself?" my dad asked.

"I'm good! You've actually come at the perfect time. We just finished cleaning from our lunch rush."

"Perfect! We would just like two cheeseburgers with all the fixings. I'll take fries, and Trevor here will have some onion rings. I want a Pepsi to go with my meal," my dad said with confidence like he had been to the place a hundred times.

"And I will take a…" The waitress interrupted me.

"I'm sorry, sir, but we only have Coke products here."

"Then I will just take a root beer." She was jotting down our order on a pad of paper and looked up at me, waiting for my response.

"And I will take a Sprite please," I said softly, quickly looking away from her glance. She turned and walked away.

"Some of these small places seem to take forever to make your food. I just hope we don't sit here and waste half our day waiting," my dad said impatiently as he was looking around the diner, checking the place out.

Not even ten minutes later she came over with our plates, set them down, and then walked back with our drinks.

"Do you gentleman need anything else?" she asked.

"Nope, everything looks just fine, thank you!" my dad replied, as he stuffed a few fries in his mouth.

We ate in silence. It didn't take long for us to finish our meals. Once we were done, our waitress came over with our check.

My dad didn't even look at the bill. He just pulled money out of his wallet, and while he was handing her the money, he said, "Miss, by chance do you know a family here in town named James, Katherine, and Nicole?"

"I'm sorry, sir, but those names don't sound familiar."

"Okay, thanks anyways, and keep the change," my dad replied.

"Thank you, sir! I hope you find who you are looking for and you both have a wonderful day!" the waitress said with a smile as she turned and walked away.

"Well, it was worth a try," Dad said. He looked deep in thought.

I broke the silence after a few minutes. "I guess we can just drive around and stop and ask at a few places, and maybe we will get lucky, Dad." The waitress started walking back over to our table.

"I don't know if this will help you at all, but I do know a girl named Nikki. I'm not sure of her last name, but she works weekends at the local ice cream shop a couple blocks from here, a place called the Cyclone. You might want to stop by there and check it out. She might be working. Maybe she is the Nicole you are looking for."

"Thanks for your help. Which direction is the ice cream shop?" My dad stood up and grabbed the car keys off the table. The waitress pointed in the direction while I took one last swig of my soda, and we were on our way.

We pulled up to the Cyclone. It was easy to spot with the big spinning ice cream cone on the edge of the parking lot. A couple of people were standing outside the take-out window.

"Feel like having an ice cream, Trevor?"

"Not really, Dad. I'm stuffed!"

We got out of the car and walked up to the window. I tried peeking through the windows to see if I could spot Nicole working, but I didn't see her. Dad and I waited in line for a few minutes while the people in front of us ordered and paid for their ice cream.

"What can I get you?" A young girl with wavy, strawberry blonde hair and crystal-blue eyes asked us.

"We are actually looking for Nicole. Is she working today?" my dad asked, glancing from side-to-side.

"She actually comes in for her shift at 4:00. Can I get you some of our world-famous huckleberry ice cream? I promise you won't be disappointed," the girl said with a reassuring smile, showing her perfectly straight, shiny white teeth that sparkled in the sunlight. She was very pretty and had a cute Kentucky accent.

"Never tried huckleberry before, but I will take your word for it. Just one scoop for me is fine. How about you, Trevor? Want to try a scoop?" My dad glanced my way.

"Sure, I think I can squeeze in one scoop!" But I knew right away I was going to regret it.

What are we going to do for the next two hours, just sit here and wait for Nicole to come in for her shift? I thought as I kicked a couple rocks.

We grabbed our ice cream and sat down at the picnic tables under a big oak tree. The leaves were starting to turn red, orange, and yellow. Fall is my favorite season. Not too hot. Not too cold. Just a beautiful time of year. I heard that the foliage in the New England states is the prettiest anywhere. I hope I can experience it for myself someday.

I took my first bite of the famous huckleberry ice cream and my taste buds burst with an intense, very unique flavor. My first choices are usually black raspberry or mint chocolate chip, but during the holidays it's peppermint stick. You can usually only buy peppermint stick in November and December, but you best stock up because they sell out fast and only have a limited supply. My mom usually picks up about ten cartons of it and stashes it in our deep freeze in the basement.

I hadn't really thought much about my mom lately, and now I thought how weird it would be when she came home. It had been kind of nice not having her around, and that thought made me feel awful for thinking that about my own mother. But it was exhausting taking care of her, keeping the house clean, finding time to do homework and going to school every day. I reminded myself it would be a completely different environment at home with no alcohol in the house and my mom completely sober. Maybe we would finally start doing things as a family again, like all the trips we used to take. Maybe when Julia got better, she could go on some trips with us.

"What's on your mind, son?" my dad said with a concerned expression.

"I was actually just thinking about Mom and how different things will be when she finally comes home."

"They will definitely be different. We can visit her tomorrow on our way home. Can you believe we haven't seen your mom in over six weeks?" my dad asked.

"I know what you mean. It's strange. I don't think I'd ever been away from Mom for an entire day since I was born until she went into rehab. But since the accident, it's like I forget anyone else exists when I'm with Julia, Mom too. I like the way she makes me feel, even when she can't hold a conversation with me. Just her presence makes my heart smile. It's hard to explain, Dad. She's just…special!" I said, feeling my cheeks getting a little warm.

"I know exactly how you feel. I felt the same way about your mother when we first met. I couldn't get enough of her. But of course, she didn't know that. I had to play it cool, hard to get."

"But why, Dad? If you liked her so much, why didn't you just tell her?"

"Well, Trevor, your mom was popular in school. She could have had any guy she wanted. I didn't want to try too hard and embarrass myself if your mother didn't like me the way I liked her. We were in the same homeroom, and we had Biology and Chemistry together, and her locker was right next to mine. So, I got to see your mom every day. I always thought she had the prettiest smile. She could light up a room when she walked in. I, on the other hand, was not popular. I was quiet and shy. I got really good grades in school and studied a lot. I wanted to get a full scholarship to go to college. I was the Salutatorian in our graduating class. Your mom was really impressed with how smart I was. She asked if we could do a science project together, and of course I agreed. Your mom was so ecstatic that we got an A+ on our project that she kissed me on the cheek. See, your mom was really bad in

Science, on the brink of flunking out of the class. After that she asked if I would come over to her place and help her with homework and to study for tests and help her with projects. And that's how it all started."

My father and I talked about everything under the sun, and before we knew it, it was almost time for Nicole, if this Nikki was in fact Nicole, to start her shift. We never talked about what we expected to happen once we broke the news to her family. We were desperate and didn't know of any other alternative for finding relatives of the Hendricks.

A light jade Subaru pulled into the parking lot and a girl resembling Nicole stepped out, but it was hard to tell for sure if it was her since the car was parked on the other side of the parking lot.

"Dad, I think that's Nicole!" I said as I stood up. We walked quickly toward the car.

"If that's her parents in the car, we need to stop them before they leave," Dad said as we started running now.

"Nicole!" I yelled. She turned around with a confused look on her face. As we got closer, Nicole recognized me.

"Trevor, is that you?" she asked, surprised. "Is Julia with you?" She brushed a strand of hair away from her eyes. My expression must have given it away because Nicole's smile turned very quickly. "What are you doing here?" she asked, confused. Both of Nicole's parents stepped out of the car. I turned to my dad because I didn't want to be the one to break the news to her. I was at a loss for words anyway. It felt like a big lump had formed in my throat.

"James, Katherine, Nicole...," my dad said with a shaky voice. "We have some terrible news! Julia and her parents were in a horrible car accident a week ago. Alex and

Janessa…were killed!" my dad choked out. "And as for Julia…she is in a coma." My dad dropped his head and wiped a tear. Nicole covered her face in her hands and started to cry uncontrollably. "I'm so sorry that we had to tell you this way. We don't know anything about the Hendricks, and we were hoping you could help us contact their family and let them know what happened. We didn't know who else to contact. I've only come to a bunch of dead ends."

There was complete silence for what seemed like eternity. I could hear the wind rustling the leaves and birds chirping in a nearby tree. I walked over to Nicole and wrapped my arms around her, trying to comfort her. She looked up at me, her eyes filled with tears, and when blinked they streamed down her cheeks like a cascading river.

A few moments later, Nicole broke the silence. "When can I see Julia?" She choked out as she wiped her cheeks. She glanced at my dad, then back at me.

"You'll have to discuss that with your parents. We are heading back first thing tomorrow morning," my dad replied. Nicole walked over to her parents and said something quietly. Her dad nodded and walked away.

Just a few minutes later he returned. "Why don't we head back to our place. We can talk this over and see if we can be of any help," James said in a slightly shaky voice.

"That sounds good. We'll follow you," my dad replied with a forced smile, and we turned and walked toward our car.

***

Three days later, Nicole and her parents were on their way to Virginia. The funeral was set for 4:00 at Bedford Funeral Home on Rock Castle Road. It took only three days to contact the Hendricks family and for them to arrange travel plans to make it to the funeral. It felt awkward meeting all their family for the first time on such a sad, unfortunate day, and I was starting to get nervous.

I wished Julia could be here. It was really sad that Julia couldn't attend her own parents' funeral, but the doctors said that she needed to be in a medically induced coma for at least two weeks due to her brain swelling.

My dad mentioned that funerals usually take place two to three days after someone dies but can sometimes wait longer depending on the travel arrangements families have to make. With head injuries, the doctor informed us, it's hard to say how long it will take Julia to wake out of her drug-induced coma. The doctor mentioned it may take several weeks, months, or in even the worst-case scenario, years for her to wake up.

After seeing photographs of the car crash in the local newspaper, I couldn't believe that Julia had survived. The car was unrecognizable—it was truly a miracle. It sent chills to the bone just thinking about it.

***

The service was nice, and Julia's parents were buried at Blue Ridge Memorials Gardens. After the service we all went together to an upscale restaurant, Luigi's Gourmet Italian Restaurant, in Roanoke. The menu was huge, with enough choices to give anyone a headache. I swear it took a good twenty minutes for everyone to finally decide on what they wanted to eat.

After dinner Julia's family left for their hotels for the night. Everyone was leaving in the early morning hours to catch their flights back home. Nicole and her parents stayed at our place for the night. We have a guest room with a private bathroom that hadn't been used in years.

We stayed up most the night, the parents in the dining room playing poker and drinking while Nicole and I sat in the living room watching a movie and eating popcorn.

The next morning Nicole and her family headed back home.

COMA

I had come to visit Julia every day for the last nine weeks. The doctor told me that the longer she stayed in a coma the greater the chances were of her waking up with brain damage. Two weeks after the accident, Dr. Harris stopped administering the medication to keep her in a coma which was enough time to stop the swelling of the brain. Her vitals remained stable, but there had been no increase in brain activity.

With both her parents dead, I'm not even sure she wanted to wake up. I only met Julia a few weeks before the accident, but I felt such a close connection to her that I hated leaving her side. I knew I couldn't do much, except sit by her bedside, hold her hand, and tell her everything was going to be okay. I talked to her as if she could hear me. I told her how school was going and how my mom was doing, just normal day to day stuff that I would talk to her about if she was coherent and could respond.

Sometimes I even paused—waiting—hoping for a response. Hoping for a two-sided conversation, but she just lay there with her eyes closed, unresponsive, not moving. All I heard was the machine that produced the oxygen to keep her alive.

Tragic Mercy

***

Each day that I visited Julia, I fell for her even more. She was so innocent, and her life had become so tragic.

My dad had been awesome through this whole ordeal. He was busy working five days a week, we visited Mom every Sunday, he even dropped me off at the hospital every day after school to visit Julia and picked me up. He knew how much she meant to me and that she had no one else right now. We also had talks about not getting too attached because even the doctors had no clue how long she would be in this coma. He also said he didn't want me throwing my life away waiting.

"There's so much you could be doing with your life right now," my dad said. "For instance, spending more time on homework or studying so you can keep your grades up in school. Even going to the arcade, you love the arcade."

But I couldn't focus even if I tried. Julia was all I could think about. "Life just isn't fair!" I told him. "She is so young and has her whole life ahead of her. And if she ever wakes up from this coma, her whole world will be completely turned upside down."

"You're right, Son. Life isn't fair." He lowered his head and let out a big sigh. "Julia doesn't deserve any of this. She is a great person and so were her parents. They were amazing people. All I can tell you, is that life can be really cruel sometimes. Your entire world can change in just a blink of an eye."

***

I get deep in thought some nights lying in bed trying to fall asleep. I think about how different things will be for Julia. How she will grow up with no parents. How they won't be there for her high school graduation or to help her through college if she decides to go. They won't be there for birthdays or holidays. They won't be there for her wedding, or the birth of any babies she may have, or see them grow up. This really breaks my heart into pieces just thinking about it. I care so much for Julia that I don't want to see her hurt. And I have a feeling she is going to hurt a lot when she wakes up.

When I was younger, my mom used to always say I was wiser than my years, that I have an old soul. I never knew what that meant, and I probably still don't understand it completely. But I have noticed that my intellect has always been high for my age, even as a child, and now as a teenager, I notice myself getting bored with school—it's not challenging enough. Also, the conversations I overhear in the hallways or at lunch are so insignificant and dull. I like to have deep conversations that have substance and meaning.

I was hoping to develop that type of relationship with Julia, but we never got the chance to spend time alone—just the two of us. How could I say that? I've spent many days alone with her, just not in the way I was hoping. She just lays there, while I do all the talking. Or I sit here, not saying a word, just watching her, admiring how beautiful she is, how sad I feel for her, and just hold her hand, trying to comfort her. She probably doesn't even know that I'm here, but that's not the point.

One particular nurse took an interest in us. Jackie, a petite woman in her thirties with amazing, translucent blue eyes, and long honey-brown hair that fell halfway down her back. Every time she worked, she made a point to check in on me and see how I was doing. She always told me how lucky Julia was to have such a caring boyfriend who loved her so much. Even though I'm technically not

Julia's boyfriend, I never corrected her. I liked being called her boyfriend; it made me smile and feel warm and tingly inside. I didn't know much about Jackie since she always slipped out of the room as quick as she slipped in, said she didn't want to disturb our time alone. But I mentioned my concern to her a couple times, that I didn't think Julia even knew I was with her. Nurse Jackie told me once that studies have proven that coma patients can hear and feel. MRI scans revealed that patients brains increased in neural activity when they heard a familiar voice call out their name, told them a story, or even when just touching them. Also, research has shown that it can help coma patients recover their consciousness faster. Hearing that gave me hope. It was reassuring to think Julia might be able to hear me, and that possibly just my presence, voice, and touch, may help her recover faster.

I wanted nothing more than for Julia to wake up, to hear her voice again, to see those big, beautiful emerald green eyes and her pearly, white smile again. But the other part of me wanted to protect her from all the pain and tears she would experience when she finally woke up from this coma. It was like a battlefield in my head, all the worries and feelings, all the "what if's." The unpredictability was giving me major anxiety. I like structure and organization. I like to plan ahead—no surprises—a set schedule. And after the accident, life was nothing but chaos. I hated not knowing. I hated the thoughts that infested my altered mind of existence now.

My schedule didn't help, being cooped up in school all day, coming directly to the hospital for a couple of hours, then on Sundays going to visit Mom. This was not what I pictured my junior year in high school being like at all. But shit happens, and I told myself to suck it up and deal with it, put my big boy pants on and stop worrying so much about the inevitable. I told myself that the only thing I could change about this situation was the way I think—my attitude. If I had more positive thoughts, those vibes might electrify through Julia's body and mind when I'm around her, which might cause a spark in her brain activity. That might be the answer to her waking from this coma. Positive thinking. Happy thoughts. That's the answer!

It was like a light bulb just went off in my head. I can't lay in bed all night thinking. I need to get some sleep. Tomorrow is a new day. I'm going to get my mind on track and dive into positive thinking right away. This is going to work. This is the key. This is why Julia hasn't woken up yet. She needs to be around people who are strong, have happy and positive attitudes to help her through these tough times. Someone to build her up emotionally and to be there for her. Someone who won't allow her to get sucked into the darkness of depression but will bring the light back into her eyes.

I could feel my mind and body relaxing and coming to peace with one another. It was exhilarating. Life can be very complicated at times, but if we can dig ourselves out of the hole, there are endless possibilities we can achieve. Much greatness to experience. Lives we can change. I could feel my eyes getting heavy as I drifted off to dreamland.

***

Two weeks later, the doctors were seeing some brain activity, nothing drastic, but definitely a step in the right direction. I really think that my positive thinking sparked something in Julia, like she could feel my inner electricity jumping through my skin when I was around her. They have been monitoring her more closely since they first noticed the change. Nurse Jackie told me the other day that the doctors could see a jump in brain activity when I visited her. She had yet to move or open her eyes that anyone knew of, but I had a good feeling about this. I truly believed Julia would finally wake up by the end of the week. I told my dad I would never forgive myself if Julia woke up and she was all alone. But my dad also made it very clear that he didn't want me to miss any more school.

I heard a gentle tapping, then my bedroom door slowly opened, and my dad poked his head around the corner. "Breakfast is ready. I tried something new. You'll have to let me know what you think," my dad said in a half whisper like he was trying to be quiet and not wake anyone, even though it was just the two of us in the house.

"It smells delicious."

My dad just smiled and turned down the hall toward the kitchen. My dad must not have slept very well. He usually made something quick before school so we could eat breakfast together, but apparently, he had something different up his sleeve this morning. I kicked my legs over the bed half asleep, then slowly walked to the kitchen dragging me feet along the way. My dad had just set both our plates on the table.

"I was flipping through the channels last night while I was having a hard time falling asleep, and I came across this cooking show. I've always wanted to try these," my dad said as he looked up at me.

"What is it?" I asked while letting out a big yawn.

"Eggs Benedict."

"Looks fancy! How long have you been cooking?"

"Just a little over an hour."

"What exactly is eggs benedict?" I asked as I sat down at the table.

"Poached eggs with broiled ham on grilled English muffins and smothered in hollandaise sauce with a side of my home fries that you like so much."

"Looks and smells amazing!" I said as I took my first fork full. The sauce was rich and buttery. I've never had a poached egg before, but it was actually really good. The yolk broke and ran down the plate, but the egg whites had a nice crust. The ham was crisp and salty. My dad loves to season everything in Lawry's. I must admit, Lawry's makes everything taste better.

"Mmmmmm. Dad, this is really good!" I said with a mouthful.

"I'm glad you like it. I think I'm going to make some crepes for breakfast tomorrow."

"Crepes?" I asked, confused.

"It's French. It's basically a real thin pancake rolled up in whatever you want, usually some sort of a fruit filling, then drizzled with maple syrup and whipped cream."

"Sounds more like dessert to me."

"Pretty much," my dad said, as he chuckled.

My dad is a good cook. I've really liked having him around. It's been hard the last couple of years with him being away all the time. But now that Mom is getting the help she needs to stop drinking, I think we can be a happy family again. At least that's what I'm hoping for.

"Better hurry up and get ready for school or you're going to be late, Trevor," my dad said as he glanced at the clock hanging on the back wall. I jumped out of the chair, set the empty plate in the sink and took a big gulp of orange juice before hurrying off to my bathroom to shower quickly. I'm glad I'm not a girl. I've heard some girls my age, take an hour or more to get ready in the morning. For me, it's less than ten minutes.

***

My dad dropped me off at the hospital right after school like always, and as he drove off, I waved but I don't think he saw me. This time everything felt different about the hospital, the people, the aura, even the temperature was off—like something wasn't right. I started to panic!

"Julia!" I gasped as I darted down the hall and around the corner to the elevators. I pressed the button to the fourth floor, but I was getting impatient waiting and ran to the staircase. I took long strides, skipping two stairs at a time, as I ran up the flight of stairs as fast as I could, almost losing my balance a few times. I grabbed a hold of the railing to keep from falling and kept moving. I made it to the fourth floor and pushed hard against the door. As it flung open, the door almost hit someone.

"Sorry!" I said quickly, as I ran past the nurses' station to Julia's room. I stood in front of the closed door for a few moments to catch my breath and regain my composure, took a deep breath in and exhaled, then pushed the door slowly open.

My eyes must be playing tricks on me, I thought. Julia was awake and sitting up in her bed. She glanced over at me while I just stood there like a statue. I couldn't speak or move. I just stood there like a complete idiot. She smiled at me. I couldn't tell if she recognized me or if it was a nervous smile, like who is this weirdo standing in my room staring at me?

"Julia! You're awake!" managed to escape my lips.

"Who are you?" Julia asked, confused.

My worst nightmare had come true, I thought. *She doesn't even remember me!*

118

My heart dropped like a bowling ball that hit the floor with a massive thud, cracking and shattering the floor around me. This can't be happening right now. I was at a loss for words. I turned around and walked out of the room. I walked to the family waiting room a few doors down and sat down in the chair because I felt like my legs were going to collapse from under me. I buried my head in my hands as warm tears streamed down my cheeks. A hard lump formed in my throat, making it almost impossible to speak, even if I wanted to. I couldn't let Julia see me like this. I had to be strong.

"Be positive," I said out loud. "Help her through this, even if she doesn't remember who I am. Dr. Harris warned me that this might happen." I was just hoping it didn't come true and she would regain consciousness like a day hadn't passed by and remembered everything like it was yesterday. But I had to face reality. And the reality was, I screamed inside my head, *SHE DOESN'T REMEMBER ME!*

MEMORIES

Other than Julia losing most of her memory, she seemed perfectly normal. After almost twelve weeks in a coma, she's gone to physical therapy four days a week for three weeks now, to help her regain strength in her legs. But worst of all, she's experiencing severe migraines. Bright lights seem to bother her the most. She wears sunglasses most of the day.

Nicole came down to visit for a weekend, but Julia doesn't remember her either, which I think crushed Nicole. I'm not sure given the distance she has to travel, if Nicole will try visiting much since Julia doesn't remember her; but only time will tell.

Even though Julia doesn't remember me, I still visit her every day. It's not like we were childhood friends or anything, I just met her a few weeks prior to the car accident, but there's definitely an intense connection drawing me to her. I'm not sure exactly what it is, but it's an undeniable force pulling me to her like a magnet. I just can't shake the feeling. It's weird and hard to describe, but all I know is this is where I'm supposed to be. Maybe this is what you hear people talk about when they say that they just know this person is, *"THE ONE!"*

I'm not sure if Julia experiences the same feelings I do, and even if she does, I don't want to force her into anything too quickly after everything she has been through. Her only focus right now should be trying to get her memory back. Some parts might come back in pieces, with a simple smell, or photo; or she might wake up one day and remember everything. The thing about the brain is that it's so unpredictable. No one knows what to expect, how long, or when—it's just a waiting game. And I'm willing to wait no matter how long it takes for her to regain her memories, and even if she doesn't, I want to make new memories with her.

Julia's Aunt Robin and Uncle Dave moved to Virginia to take care of her. From what I understand, Julia's parents had really big life insurance policies. In the case that both of them died, Julia gets everything. I'm not exactly sure how much, and really, it's none of my business, but it sounds like she'll never have to work a day in her life if she doesn't want to.

I was sitting next to Julia, admiring her beauty as she was flipping through old photo albums her mother had put together of their family since she was a baby. There was a big stack of albums, and Julia was hoping that looking through them, would spark some sort of memory; but as she flipped through the pages, she was getting more and more frustrated. I felt helpless. I didn't know what to say or do to comfort her. I can't imagine what she was going through. Her life was like a book full of blank pages—her entire existence a mystery waiting to be solved.

"I don't understand why this isn't helping me remember anything?" Julia said harshly as she slammed the photo album shut and buried her face in her hands.

I didn't know what to say, so I just rubbed her back. "It's going to be okay, Julia. Your body and mind have gone through a lot the last few months. It's probably just on overload right now. Maybe instead of trying to force yourself to remember, just take it slow, day by day, and it might come back to you over time," I replied calmly.

"I know, but it's just so frustrating! You have no idea what it's like to wake up and not remember anyone or anything!" Julia said on the verge of tears.

"I'm not even going to try to pretend like I have any idea what you're going through right now. It's heartbreaking to see you like this Julia, and I wish I had some magical words that would just make this all go away! I just want to see you smile again. You have a beautiful smile." I could feel my cheeks turning red.

"Thanks, Trevor. You're sweet," Julia said as she looked up at me with a half-smile. I looked away shyly. There's so much I just wanted to tell her, but I couldn't. I didn't want to scare her away. She had enough emotions to deal with. We sat there in silence for a while.

"Are you hungry?" I asked, breaking the silence.

"A little bit," Julia replied, twiddling her thumbs.

"What are you in the mood for?"

She sat there with her legs crossed, deep in thought. "I've actually been craving one of those smothered burritos at the Mexican food truck in Redwood." Julia's eyes became wide and she just sat there for a minute and didn't say anything. "OH MY!" she gasped. "How did I remember that?"

"That was your favorite place to go this summer when Nicole was staying with you, when we first met."

"Wow! That was so weird!" Julia said as she rubbed her temples. "It just came out of nowhere. This is amazing! I actually remembered something!" Julia said with excitement in her voice.

"Do you remember the dessert we would always order and share after the burrito?" I asked, trying to pry in that little mind of hers a bit more.

Julia closed her eyes, took a deep breath and held it for a few moments, then let it out slowly. Her eyes flew wide open. "Fried ice cream with honey."

"That's right, is there anything else you can remember?" I asked.

"Not at the moment," she let out a heavy sigh.

"That's a great start, Julia. This is just the beginning. Maybe your memories will just come back to you when you least expect it," I said with a reassuring tone.

"I really hope so, Trevor. You have no idea what it's like not remembering anything."

This is my chance to start a new life, to new beginnings with people who care about me. I trust Trevor, he makes me feel good when I'm around him. There's something about him. These happy thoughts put my busy mind at ease.

THE
WILLIAMS

An alarm sounded loudly. I darted into the kitchen and found my dad standing on a chair, frantically waving a dish towel in front of the smoke detector, trying to get the smoke alarm to stop beeping. The smoke just hung in the air like a thick fog.

"Trevor, can you open up a window!" my dad yelled over the top of the screeching alarm. I ran to the closest window but the lock was hard to turn, like it had been painted shut. I gave it a hard pull but with no luck. "Trevor! Any day now!" my dad yelled from across the room.

"Dad! I'm trying. It's stuck." I tried it again, and this time it turned. I pushed open the window and ran over to the front door and waved the door back and forth trying to clear the air of the smoke. The alarm finally stopped, and my dad jumped down from the chair with a thud.

"What's burning?" I asked.

"Dinner!" my dad replied with frustration as he opened the stove door and more smoke came barreling out. "The grease from the meatloaf must have overflowed." He slowly pulled the meatloaf out of the oven, set it on top of the stove, and more grease spilled out. "What a mess," my dad said, annoyed. "Doesn't look like the meatloaf got burned, but it probably tastes like smoke, ugh! How would you feel about going out and getting a bite to eat instead, Trevor?"

"Sounds good to me, Dad."

"Maybe by the time we get back the house will be aired out from all the smoke. Let's just open a few more windows before we leave."

***

"What are you in the mood for Trevor?" my dad asked as he backed the car out of the driveway.

"We haven't been to that new Hibachi Grill that just opened in town a few weeks ago. I heard the chef cooks the food right in front of you. I overheard the kids at school talking about the place. They said they put on quite a show, with lots of cool tricks. The Japanese chefs throw a bunch of knives, do some sort of egg juggling, and make a volcano out of onions."

"Sounds like a lot of fun. Let's try the place out."

The place was packed, and we had to wait twenty minutes before getting seated. I was beyond starved at this point, and I was anxious to see all these cool tricks I'd been hearing about in school.

We got seated at a table with a bunch of strangers, which was a little odd, but it wasn't long before the entertainment started. The chef walked over to the table and squirted sake on the hot stove which sent flames shooting high to the ceiling. He continued to do a bunch of tricks with knives, throwing them high up while they were spinning, catching them and throwing them around his back. Then he did a few tricks involving eggs. The chef tossed the egg back and forth between two metal spatulas and then flipped it in the front pocket of his shirt. He took another egg and spun it around on the hot grill and tossed it up with a spatula into his tall chef hat before cracking them over the grill. Then preceded to make egg fried rice in the shape of a big heart. The chef then layered rings of an onion on top of each other, largest ring on bottom to the smallest on top, to make a volcano with shooting flames through the top. I decided I definitely wanted to take Julia here sometime.

"THAT'S IT!" I yelled.

"What's it?" my dad asked, confused.

"Sorry! Did I say that out loud?" I snickered. "I've just been wracking my brain about something special to do for Julia—you know—to take her mind off everything. I should take her zip-lining and then to the Hibachi Grill for dinner afterward. I think she would have so much fun," I said cheerfully.

"I think that's a great idea!"

I remembered doing the same thing right before the accident. Uncertain what to do the day Julia and I were supposed to be alone for the first time. I remembered thinking at work, right after Julia and her parents left Taco Bell, that I really wanted to take her zip-lining.

When we got home and walked through the front door the smell of smoke was hardly noticeable. My dad walked over to the answering machine since the red light was blinking—alerting us that there was a message waiting. Not many people call the house line, except Mom's doctor at the treatment center.

Hi Mr. Williams. This is Dr. Harrington. I'm sorry to bother you this late in the evening, but I was busy in meetings all day. I just wanted you to know that I have approved your wife's release from our clinic. If you show up around 2:00 on Sunday, we should have all the documents ready for you to sign. If you have any questions, please feel free to call the office.

My dad just stood there in disbelief. I wasn't sure if he was excited or upset. It was hard to read him. I broke the silence. "Dad, that's great! Mom finally gets to come home!"

"I know," my dad paused. "It's fantastic."

He didn't seem very happy.

***

I heard a gentle tapping on my door. I opened my eyes and glanced at my digital alarm clock, sitting on the nightstand next to my bed. It read 8:35.

"Trevor? You awake? Breakfast is ready," my dad said quietly.

"Yeah, Dad. Just give me a minute," I replied half asleep—my throat dry as sandpaper. I could hear my dad walk away from my door and down the hall.

As I walked into the kitchen, my dad had just finished setting the table. He had made waffles, fried eggs, and sausage links for breakfast. I walked to the cabinet and pulled out a glass, then poured myself a glass of orange juice as my dad was topping off his coffee. I dragged my slippers across the floor because I was too lazy to pick my feet up. I let out a big yawn and sat down at the table across from my dad. I reached for the strawberries. My dad was cutting up strawberries last night before we went to bed. He said if you generously coat the strawberries in a bunch of sugar, then leave it in the refrigerator overnight, the natural juices from the strawberries get drawn out, making it perfect for drizzling over waffles the next morning.

I love strawberries. My mom makes the best homemade strawberry jam. It's been years since she made it, but now that she's coming home and is better, maybe she will start doing some of the stuff she used to do before she started drinking too much. I really hoped things go back to the way they were before the alcohol took control of her life, when we used to be happy and enjoy each other's company. I really hoped my mom could stay away from the booze this time. Otherwise, I'm afraid she'll drive my father away again.

My dad was quiet during breakfast. He didn't say much. I knew he must be deep in thought, and maybe worried about Mom coming home today. I stood up from the table, grabbed my dirty dishes and set them in the sink.

My dad finally spoke up. "I would like to leave by 9:30 at the latest."

"No problem, Dad! I just have to jump in the shower, and I'll be ready." I walked toward my bedroom and closed the door behind me.

***

There was an awkward silence the entire four-hour drive to pick up Mom. You would think we would be excited that she was coming home, but something wasn't quite right. The silence and long drive had me deep in thought.

Maybe Dad doesn't love Mom anymore. Maybe even if she does stop drinking for good, it won't fix what has been done. We are a broken family and maybe we can't be fixed.

I just hoped that once he saw Mom his heart would change. I knew my mom still had a lot of work to prove herself, but it was possible. *Miracles do happen*, I told myself.

I know this cost my dad a lot of money to put her into this treatment program. I overheard my dad talking on the phone one night with his brother Joe. He said something about how the insurance covered a majority of the bill, but he will have to pay the rest out of pocket, which was about twenty grand.

Maybe he's afraid Mom is beyond help and she's wasted all the money he'd spent putting her in the most prestigious program... Stop! I shook my head. *Who was I kidding? I can't read minds.* All this silence and over-thinking was going to make me insane. I needed to break the silence.

"Dad?"

"Yes, Trevor?"

"Do you think Mom is better?" I asked quietly, like I was a child afraid to speak.

My dad took a deep breath. "I don't know. I really hope so. Dr. Harrington seems to think she is better and can come home. So we need to trust his professional opinion."

"I know, Dad. It just seems like you're distant and deep in thought. I don't know what to think right now. We should be happy that Mom's coming home today, but it seems like you're upset about it." I lowered my head.

"It's complicated, Trevor. Adult issues are something you shouldn't be worried about. You should be hanging out with your friends, going on dates with Julia, and having fun! Instead, you overthink and worry about everyone else." He quickly looked in my direction—his eyes sad. "Your mom was right when she said you have an old soul. You're just too smart for your own good!" He shoved me playfully. A smile finally escaped his lips.

"I'll take that as a compliment," I smirked.

TREVOR
&
JULIA

"I'm glad I finally get to meet your mom," said Julia.

"I'm going to warn you, my mom is a talker. We'll get trapped at my house for hours if you let her."

"Don't worry so much, Trevor. If we get talking, it's not the end of the world. How about this? If your mom and I have talked for more than an hour, just give me a little nudge or speak up and we can take off. Okay?"

"Yeah, sounds good," I said with a half-smile. "I'm going to be honest with you, Julia. I'm really nervous about you meeting my mom. She was a complete and total mess five months ago. My parents were on the verge of getting a divorce. My dad would disappear for days at a time, and so, my mom thought he was having an affair.

She had a serious drinking problem—a severe alcoholic. To the point that alcohol controlled every aspect of her life. She stopped taking care of herself. She went into a deep depression. She would go days without showering, and she put on over a hundred pounds in less than five years. She stopped cooking and cleaning.

She would start to drink the moment she woke up. By the time I got home from school, she would be passed out on the couch, sometimes covered in puke and her drink spilled over on the carpet. I never invited any friends over because I was embarrassed. I didn't want kids whispering and pointing fingers in the hall, making fun of me. It's hard enough going to high school with all the rumors that spread like wildfire. I didn't need something like this to add to it."

"It's okay, Trevor. Your mom is better now. She hasn't drunk in over five months! That's a real accomplishment. You should be proud of her! I've heard that alcoholism is an extremely hard habit to break. It destroys families and lives every day," Julia replied sympathetically.

"I know firsthand how true that is. I lived in a nightmare. I felt so hopeless. I tried my best to take care of my mom, the house, and myself since I was twelve." I shifted uncomfortably. "I managed to go to school and get good grades. My dad's big on education, but he traveled a lot for work. He would be gone for weeks at a time, leaving me alone to take care of my mother." I glanced at the floor then back up at Julia. "I just hope she never takes a sip of alcohol again."

"I am so sorry you had to go through that, Trevor. That must have been hard on you. I can't imagine what it was like for you growing up." Julia sniffled, and placed her hand on my knee and wiped away a tear with her other hand. "I had an easy childhood. No hardships like you experienced. I was able to be a kid and have no worries in life." Julia lowered her head. I think she felt bad for even saying it.

"Don't get me wrong. Before my mom had a drinking problem, we were a happy family. We used to go on family vacations—trips all over the world. I don't know what happened to us or why my mom started drinking so much, except that she suspected that my father was cheating on her when he was away on his business trips. Instead of confronting my dad about her concerns, she just drank to take the pain away and to make herself feel better. She turned to alcohol to comfort herself. That's when it started to become a serious problem. She stopped caring about everything and everyone, even me."

A hard lump formed in the back of my throat and I tried to choke back my tears. Julia leaned over and gave me a big hug. She squeezed tight and didn't let go for a long time. I felt such a strong connection between us.

A door slammed shut and startled me. "My mom and dad must be home from grocery shopping. Let's give them a few minutes to put the groceries away, and then we can join them in the other room," I said, trying to regain my composure.

"Yeah, of course," Julia replied with a smile that.

***

"Tammy. I think it's time you let Trevor and Julia get to where they were planning on going today," my dad finally interrupted.

"I'm just enjoying Julia's company. This is the first time we've met, and I'm just trying to get to know the girl is all," my mom replied.

"But you've been doing most of the talking, my love," he said as he raised both of his eyebrows.

"You know, Julia, Trevor really adores you! He talks about you all the time," my mom said, glancing over at Julia and then at me.

"Mom!" I said, gritting my teeth.

"Isn't he so cute when he's embarrassed?" my mom asked.

"Okay honey, now let's leave these two alone." My dad stood up and held out his hand to my mom. "Let's go into the kitchen and discuss what we are going to make for our romantic dinner date tonight.

"Okay, okay!" my mom said as she got up from the recliner.

"It was really nice to finally meet you, Julia."

"Nice to meet you too, Mrs. Williams," Julia said as she stood up and shook my mom's hand.

"You don't have to be all formal with me, my dear. Give me a hug!" my mom said as she reached for Julia. "You two have fun!" my mom said as she followed my dad into the kitchen.

I looked over at Julia. "You ready to go now?"

"Sure am. What do you have planned for us for the day, or are you keeping it a secret?" Julia asked as she ran her fingers through her long, silky, honey blonde hair.

"I want it to be a surprise, so I'm not going to tell you. You'll just have to wait and see," I replied with a big grin.

"So, what are you waiting for? Let's get going!" Julia said cheerfully as she grabbed her purse and followed me out the door.

***

We pulled up to Mountain Lake Treetop Adventures. "What's this place?" Julia asked curiously.

"You ready for an adrenaline kick?" I asked, psyched.

"I'm not so sure," Julia replied with a little caution in her voice.

"We're going to have so much fun! Just trust me," I said as I grabbed her hand and led her down the trail to the office. I glanced back at Julia, and she had a grin from ear to ear.

We approached the counter. "Can I help you?" a lady with short dark hair and a pointy nose asked.

"Yes, we would like two for the zip-line tour," I replied.

"What exactly are we doing?" Julia asked as she glanced at me.

The lady behind the counter spoke up. "You will walk over sky bridges, swings, rope ladders, and zip-line through the forest. It really is exhilarating! Are you the super adventurous types or would you like the less challenging course?" she asked us.

I looked at Julia, waiting for her response. She took a deep breath, "I feel like living on the edge today, so let's take the more challenging course!" Julia replied with a nervous smile.

"You sure, Julia? We can take the less challenging one if you want to," I replied.

"I feel like being a daredevil today! I was in a coma for three months. I need some excitement in my life!"

***

We spent two hours of the most fun I've ever had, and Julia was having the time of her life. I don't think she wanted to leave, but our time was over, and I was getting hungry.

"So, how did you like it?" I asked Julia.

"Trevor, that was soooo much fun! We have to do that again!!!" she said, giddy as a kid on Christmas morning. I just smiled.

"Are you hungry?" I asked.

"Starved!"

"Good. I have the perfect place in mind."

We pulled up to the New Hibachi Grill. It was 4:25, a little early for dinner but we were both ravenous. Best of all we beat the dinner rush and there was no waiting. We got seated right away. There was a cute elderly couple holding hands at the other side of the table from us. They had to be in their eighties. I wondered what their secret was, being so happy after so many years together?

Julia glanced over the menu for a few minutes, then set it down on the table just as the chef approached and the entertainment began. I kept glancing at Julia, her beautiful, contagious smile. She was mesmerized by all the fascinating tricks. Her eyes got big every time the flame shot up like a volcano. The food was fantastic, and I think Julia was enjoying every second of it. She turned her head and glanced at me with smiling eyes.

"Are you ready for some fried ice cream?" I asked her.

"Are you kidding me? Of course I am!" We split the ice cream and headed back to the car after I paid the bill.

I drove Julia back to her house and gazed up through the windshield at the millions of stars that lit the dark night like diamond dust. The air was crisp and the sky clear. The radiant full moon shone bright as the constellations danced through the sky on this most magical night. *I couldn't be any happier than I was right now*, I thought.

I pulled into Julia's driveway and parked the car. Julia leaned toward me and put her hand on my knee.

"Trevor, I just wanted you to know that I had the most amazing day ever! I don't remember ever being this happy before. I don't want this day to end." She closed her eyes and leaned in for a kiss. Her lips were soft and sweet, I never wanted this moment to end.

I was falling deeply in love with Julia and could only hope she felt the same way. I glanced up and saw a shooting star fall from the sky and disappear into the distant silent night.

THE
SURPRISE

So much had changed. It was four years ago when we first kissed under that shooting star. We had graduated high school; I was getting my engineering degree at Ferrum College and Julia a nursing degree. Julia's Aunt and Uncle moved back to their hometown in Mississippi, and I moved in with Julia.

My mom still hadn't had a drop of alcohol and I couldn't be more proud of her. She had lost almost a hundred pounds and was back to the size she was when my parents first got married. They were like newlyweds again, very affectionate and playful. They couldn't keep their hands off each other.

***

I had just got home from taking exams all day and was mentally exhausted. As I walked through the front door, the tantalizing aromas of dinner danced through the air. I walked into the kitchen where my beautiful fiancé was cooking an extravagant meal. I peeked around the corner. The table was set with our finest china and lit candles. I couldn't help but wonder what the special occasion was. Julia loved to cook, but this was definitely out of the ordinary.

I walked up behind her and whispered in her ear, "What's the special occasion sweetheart?" I brushed her hair aside with my fingers and kissed her neck lightly.

Julia turned around and gave me a seductive smile, then wrapped her fingers around my neck and pulled me in for a passionate kiss. When she pulled away, she said, "I have some great news to tell you, my love! But first, can you please pull the bun out of the oven?" Julia turned to mash the potatoes. I pulled open the bottom drawer with the hot pads, and grabbed the pan, with one bun on it. A little confused, I set it on top of the stove.

"Why just a single roll? Have you decided to cut bread out of your diet?" I asked.

"No, silly." Julia giggled. "That's the surprise!"

"Am I missing something here? Because I am really confused right now," I asked, perplexed.

"You've never heard the expression a bun in the oven?" Julia teased.

"No. I guess I must be behind the times. What does it mean?"

"We're pregnant!" Julia exclaimed, and she ran over and gave me a big hug.

"We're having a baby?!" I replied excitedly. I grabbed Julia by the waist, spun her around, and gave her a big smooch. "How far along are you?"

"I'm not sure exactly. I just took a pregnancy test this morning. I was a week late. My cycle has been off by a day or two before, but never an entire week. So, I decided to pick up a test. I will call the doctor's office tomorrow and make an appointment."

"I can't wait to tell Mom and Dad!" I blurted.

***

Five months later, Julia had just barely started to show a little baby bump. We had discussed getting married before the baby was born when Julia first found out she was pregnant. We didn't want to rush into marriage, but the pregnancy definitely hurried things along. Besides, Julia stressed the fact that she did not want to have to wear a maternity wedding gown.

After five months of planning, the wedding was right around the corner. We decided to have a small wedding, nothing too extravagant. We sent out wedding invitations to twenty people. Besides my parents, we invited Nicole and her parents, Julia's Aunt Robin and Uncle Dave, and a few other close relatives on both sides.

We decided to have the wedding right on the lake, a beautiful spot that was literally right in our back yard. The reception would be held at our house since we have plenty of room to accommodate twenty people. We hired a local chef, Bryan Valentino, to cater our wedding. He won an award for one of the World's 50 Best Restaurants, receiving three stars, the highest Michelin accolade. A local newspaper article was published last year regarding a visit to the Horizon by Justin Gold, a famous food critic for the New York Times. He referred to the chef as a genius, and he said of the restaurant: *it has exceptional cuisine and is worth the special trip. It was an incredible dish. The meat was cooked to ultimate perfection. It had wonderful flavor, with a perfect layer of crisp on the outside and moist, juiciness on the inside.*

He gave the restaurant 3.6 stars, which is huge in the food industry. The Horizon went from being a pretty busy place on the weekends with usually an hour wait on average, to an extremely busy restaurant every day of the week, requiring reservations days in advance. We had to pay a pretty penny to have him cater our wedding, but we both felt it was well worth the money.

***

The weather forecast the morning of our wedding was for partly cloudy skies with a high of seventy-four degrees. Beautiful, in other words. Family flew in the previous day from all over the country to attend the wedding. Since the tradition is not to see the bride before the ceremony, my dad suggested I stay at their house last night.

While Julia was out with Nicole, the bridesmaid, at some upscale salon downtown getting manicures, pedicures, hair and makeup done professionally, we decided to drive to our house and set up all the chairs while we waited for the arbor to be delivered for the ceremony. The arbor was made of branches, vines, and the most vibrant flowers arranged in a delicately sophisticated style. It would be perfect to recite our wedding vows and to take pictures under. Our backyard looked straight out of a storybook.

By the time everyone arrived and was seated in the chairs surrounding our immaculately designed garden. Julia's Uncle Dave started playing Pachelbel's "Canon in D" on his acoustic guitar as Julia followed the flagstone walkway through the garden toward the arbor, where I was already standing. Julia looked absolutely stunning in her pearl white, flowing designer wedding dress. The layers fell in such way that it created a light and heavy effect simultaneously, and it had a decorative floral lace top with a plunging neckline. Julia looked like she had just stepped out of a modeling magazine.

I felt like the luckiest man in the world. I had the most stunning wife, a beautiful house on a lake, and a baby on the way. I couldn't be happier.

When she at last stood at my side, we said our vows. "I take you to be my best friend, my faithful partner, and my one true love. I promise to encourage you and inspire you, to love you truly through good times and bad. I will forever be there to laugh with you, to lift you up when you are down, and to love you unconditionally through all of our adventures in life together," I said as I slid the wedding ring on Julia's finger.

Just then, dark clouds rolled in fiercely, and a bolt of lightning hit a tree directly above us, sending sparks tumbling down upon us as we ducked and covered our hands over our heads. A second later, the loudest sonic boom of thunder erupted as the skies opened its fury upon us, and rain surged out like a tidal wave. The wind whipped around us furiously, knocking chairs over, and the arbor toppled over almost knocking me out. The violent crashing waves on the lake were flooding the beach just a few hundred feet from where we were standing. Everyone began to panic—screaming in fear, as we ran to the house as quickly as we could. Just as everyone made it inside, the power went out and we stood in darkness listening to the horrifying storm as it destroyed our perfect day.

THE BABY

Such a beautiful day destroyed within a blink of an eye, and just as quickly as it started, it stopped. The dark clouds faded, the wind calmed, and the sun shined vividly again. It made me wonder if the storm was an act of God. Was he angry that Julia and I had gotten married? I don't know how else to explain what had happened to us that day. The instant I put the ring on Julia's finger, the storm erupted without warning, violent and ferocious. But it was silly of me to even think. Julia and I were perfect for each other. I promised myself not to think about it again, but it was easier said than done. The thought just hovered over me like a dark cloud. And ever since that day three months ago, I'd had a terrible feeling, like something horrible was going to happen, and I just couldn't shake it.

***

Julia was seeing her OB/GYN once a week now, her due date just a few days away. She'd been having a difficult time sleeping at night, and I swore she got up to pee every half hour. She said the second she lay down the baby starts bouncing around, but I loved feeling the baby kick and squirm around in Julia's belly. Sometimes it looked like an alien trying to escape, creepy but cool at the same time.

We decided to keep the gender of the baby a surprise until it was born. We had names picked out. If it's a girl, Isabella Janessa, and if it's a boy, Lincoln Alexander. Julia wanted to give the baby her parent's name as their middle name in remembrance, and I really liked the idea.

***

I was awakened from a sound sleep by a bone-chilling scream of agony.

"What's wrong Julia?" I cried out.

"The baby! Something is wrong with the baby!" Julia shouted.

Adrenaline and fear pulsated through my body. I couldn't speak. It was like my voice box had been ripped out. I grabbed Julia out of bed and carried her as she continued to scream in pain.

Although I don't recall the drive, we got to the hospital within no time. A nurse rushed over with a wheelchair as soon as she saw me walk through the doors holding Julia in my arms. Julia was drenched in sweat and I don't think she ever stopped screaming. It's a hopeless feeling not being able to help your wife. It felt like I was in a dream— a nightmare really. I was there but at the same time it felt like I wasn't. My perception of reality was distorted.

This can't be real. I'm going to wake up in bed next to Julia and everything is going to be fine.

I followed the nurse in a hypnotic trance through the emergency room door and down the hall as a voice echoed over the intercom. *Dr. Meyer to the operating room.* When we reached the operating room, I was told I couldn't go in as the door slammed shut. I began pacing back and forth. A feeling of extreme nausea swept over me and frantically looked for the closest restroom. I started to feel lightheaded and dizzy. My head felt like it was going to split in two, and my heart felt as if it was going to jump right out of my chest. Everything around me started to spin as the room swallowed me into a dark abyss.

I opened my groggy eyes. Staring up at the ceiling, I was blinded by the bright florescent light that buzzed above me. I gasped loudly as if being awakened from a bad dream. Unsure how long I had been out.

"Julia!" I screamed, jumped out of the hospital bed and frantically run out the door and down the hall. Panicking, I tried to find anyone who could tell me what was going on.

Once I reached the nurses' station just around the corner, I demanded, "Where is my wife?!"

"Sir, calm down," the lady behind the counter said as she stood up from her seat. "What is your wife's name?"

"Julia Williams," I replied.

"How long have I been out?" I continued.

"What's your name, sir?" she asked.

"Trevor Williams. I brought my pregnant wife in, and they wouldn't let me in the operating room. I must have passed out!"

"Let me see what I can find out for you, Sir. Just hold on for a few minutes. I will be back."

Ten or fifteen minutes had passed when the nurse walked toward me with someone beside her. As they approached, the gentleman introduced himself.

"Mr. Williams, I'm Dr. Meyer, your wife's surgeon. Will you please follow me so we can have some privacy?" I nodded as I followed the doctor. He walked into an empty room and closed the door behind us. "Mr. Williams, I wanted to congratulate you on the birth of your beautiful baby girl. She was born at 3:02 a.m. We did everything we possibly could to save your wife, but unfortunately, we

144

couldn't stop the bleeding. She experienced what we call postpartum hemorrhaging from a ruptured blood vessel and she lost an enormous amount of blood. She went into shock, which caused cardiac arrest. We tried reviving her, but it was too late."

A feeling of unfathomable despair hit me like a freight train. My entire existence had been turned completely upside down. Just a few hours ago, Julia was lying in bed next to me and now she was dead.

JULIA IS DEAD!!! How could this be happening?

A thick static surrounded me. The doctor's voice became faint as it echoed off into the near distance of my consciousness. Everything around me became fuzzy and my perception of time was distorted. Time seemed to slow down as gravity grasped my limber body. My body collapsed as I was swallowed into the realm of darkness.

***

"Trevor, Trevor, wake up," my dad repeated as he shook me.

I slowly opened my eyes, but this time hoped to wake up from this terrible nightmare. My mom and dad were standing over me, and they had such sadness in their eyes. *This was my life now—a living nightmare.* I wondered if this was how Julia felt after she woke up from her coma and found out that her parents were dead? I wished that I too had forgotten everything—my memories wiped clean. I felt as if my head was under water and I was being suffocated while all my hopes and dreams were sucked into a powerful whirlpool of depression and misery. The cards in life I was dealt was showing hearts just hours ago, and now I have been left with a losing hand.

"Trevor, I'm so sorry," my mom said as she sobbed uncontrollably between words. My dad tried his best to keep his composure. I knew he was trying to stay strong for of us. But the eyes never lie. They were filled with sadness, and when he looked away, he wiped away a tear.

My dad cleared his throat. "Trevor, I know you are hurting terribly right now, but have you gone in to see your daughter yet?" He choked a little after those last words. I was so caught up in my emotions that I had forgotten about my daughter, Isabella. "I know how hard this has got to be for you right now, but you have to be strong for your little girl. She needs you right now," my dad said, trying to hold back tears.

I mustered up everything I had in me to stand up. My legs felt like Jell-O, wobbling and unsteady. I grabbed a hold of my dad's shoulder to keep my balance. I nodded, and my father nodded back, establishing a silent understanding as I followed my parents out of the room.

As we approached the nursery, I gazed through the large picture window at all the babies lying in their beds. A nurse approached us. "Which one is yours?" she asked.

"Isabella Williams," I answered. She glanced at the hospital band around my wrist to verify my name, walked over to a baby swaddled in a pink blanket and a tiny pink cap.

"Isabella, say hi to your daddy," the nurse said with a big smile as she handed my daughter to me for the first time. I took Isabella from her and cradled her in my arms. I looked into her bright, blue eyes and my heart just melted. I can't explain the feeling that overcame me at that moment, but I was completely overwhelmed with love, joy, and sorrow all at the same time. This fragile little angel I had to protect and love unconditionally was the sweetest, most adorable baby I could ever imagine. I know it sounds cliché, but it was definitely love at first sight. This little girl already had me wrapped around those tiny little fingers of hers, and I was perfectly okay with that.

ISABELLA

Five Years Later

It was a real struggle trying to raise Isabella without Julia around. My parents helped as much as they could. But unfortunately, Isabella had a heart condition called cardiomyopathy. We spent many days and nights at the doctor's office, hospital, and emergency room.

Cardiomyopathy is a disease of the heart muscle. It causes the heart muscle to become stiff, which makes it difficult to pump enough blood to the rest of the body. Her heart had weakened tremendously over the last several months. Isabella was placed on an organ waiting list after her doctor performed a biopsy. He removed a tiny piece of tissue from her heart to take a closer look.

Unfortunately, Isabella's rare blood type meant that finding a donor would be a challenge, and because she was only five, finding a heart small enough would be even more difficult. We were told that Isabella could be on the waiting list for years, and with her condition worsening, she might not live much longer. I'd already lost Julia and couldn't stand the thought of losing my daughter too.

I'd been doing a lot of thinking lately. Although I didn't know much about Julia's family history, I'd hoped if I looked hard enough, I would find something left behind by Julia's parents that might have some answers, or at least point me in the right direction. Julia, even years after her parents passed away, refused to throw anything away.

Most of Julia's parents' belongings were stored in the attic. I'd never gone through their things out of respect for the dead—it just didn't feel right—but now that Isabella's heart condition was worsening, I had to do everything possible to help her. I would donate my own heart, but unfortunately, I have a different blood type.

My first concern was to find out what we could on my side of the family, and since I'm adopted, my parents were doing everything to find out about my biological parents. Initially, we thought that would be impossible since it was a closed adoption and the records were sealed. But to our advantage, we found out that under our circumstances, we could get the records unsealed, but that it was a long process.

My parents had a petition form mailed to us from the county court in the county I was born in. I filled it out and sent it back. All we could do now was wait for a court date with the judge to present my case to get the adoption unsealed.

As for Julia's side of the family, I began my search right away. I walked into the attic where the temperature had climbed nearly twenty degrees. It was hot, sticky, and smelled musty. I crinkled my nose in disgust. I started rummaging through the many neatly stacked boxes. I must've been up there for at least three hours and didn't find anything that would remotely help in any way. I became very frustrated and needed a break. Just as I was walking back toward the staircase, my foot fell through a board and landed on another hard surface approximately a foot below. I slowly pulled my foot out and then pulled away the broken and loose boards. I peeked my head inside but couldn't see anything because it was too dark. I grabbed the flashlight I had left on the floor and shone the light down inside. Nothing but cobwebs were down there. I looked the other direction and that's when I saw a small container of some sort. I tried to grab it, but it was out of reach. So I ripped up a few more boards to get to it. I finally got a good grip on it, pulled it into the light and blew off all the dust that it had collected over the years. The box was locked, so I had to find something to break it open. I hoped this was worth all the trouble and not another dead end.

I hit the lock a few times with a hammer and it broke open. Inside the box was a bunch of papers which looked worn and old. To my surprise, it was a certificate of adoption. Another was an amended birth certificate. Julia was adopted?! I was shocked. There's no way Julia knew anything about this—she thought Alex and Janessa were her biological parents. As I sat on the attic floor trying to wrap my head around the information I stumbled upon, I realized this had become way more difficult than I had imagined. Everyone named on these papers were deceased. I could only hope that my marriage certificate would grant me access to some information about Julia's biological parents.

***

Three weeks passed and we were on our way to Clear Lake, South Dakota to present my case in front of the judge to unseal my adoption records. The hearing was scheduled tomorrow morning at 8:30. We flew into Sioux

Falls, South Dakota. It was the closest airport but was still ninety minutes from where we needed to be. We stayed at a hotel just a few blocks from the courthouse with a swimming pool so that Isabella could swim and splash around.

The morning came quickly, and we were waiting at the courthouse to be called by the judge. We waited for over an hour before my name had been called. I approached the stand.

"Mr. Williams, I understand you are here to petition your closed adoption records to be unsealed," The judge bellowed.

"Yes, your Honor," I replied.

"You do realize that closed adoptions are sealed for a reason?" the Judge asked.

"Yes, your Honor, I'm completely aware."

"Mr. Williams could you please address the court and explain your reasoning behind wanting these records unsealed."

"Your Honor, the only reason I want my adoption records unsealed is so that I can access medical information that may save my daughter's life. My daughter Isabella is five. She was diagnosed with a heart condition called cardiomyopathy, and she is on the organ waiting list. She must have a heart transplant, or she will die. My wife died during childbirth, and both her parents were killed in a car accident almost ten years ago. My daughter has a rare blood type and she may be on the donor waiting list for years. I know I was adopted and would like to access medical records due to dozens of diseases and medical conditions being identified as genetically inherited. Finding my birth family could save my daughter's life," I replied as I wiped the tears that had run down my cheek.

The judge sat there without saying a word, which made me nervous. After a few moments, he spoke up. "Mr. Williams, I am very sorry for your loss and it's heartbreaking to hear that your daughter is very sick. Due to her condition, I will grant that your records be unsealed so that you can find the answers you are looking for."

"Thank you, your Honor."

It took us all day, but we were able to get a court order to access my original birth certificate at the State Registrar of Vital Records. We also went to South Dakota Department of Social Services to obtain my adoption records. My birth mother's name is Natalie Hamlin, but there was no name for my birth father, which I was informed is very common in adoptions. To my surprise I am a twin, which is pretty cool. I have a sister somewhere out there that I have never met before, but I'm sure it's going to be a real challenge to find her. There was an address for my birth mother, but who knows if she still lived there because it had been twenty-five years. But it was worth a try. We decided to go back to the hotel room to relax. It had been a very long emotional day. We will try to track down my birth mother tomorrow.

I was super nervous as I drove to the house alone. My parents stayed with Isabella. We thought it would be best to not overwhelm my biological mother. If she still lived there, she's going to be shocked to find me on her doorstep. I wondered why she had my adoption sealed in the first place. I pulled up to the house, which was a nice house, but the lawn hadn't been mowed in a while. I sat in the car on the side of the road for several minutes. The palms of my hands were sweaty, and I took a couple deep breaths to calm my nerves.

"You can do this," I said out loud as reassurance. I stepped out of the car and walked toward the front door, my heart pounding in my chest. I knocked on the door and waited patiently. I waited a couple minutes, but no one came to the door. I knocked again, but louder this time. I heard a couple thumps from inside. I took a deep breath. The door opened slowly. A much older lady stood in the doorway.

"Can I help you?" the lady asked quietly.

"Yes. I'm looking for Natalie Hamlin. Does she still live here?"

"I'm sorry, but Natalie died twenty-five years ago," the lady said with sadness in her eyes. I just stood there, frozen. I didn't know what to say. "Can I ask how you know of Natalie?" she questioned.

"My name is Trevor. I'm her son." I replied shyly. The lady's eyes widened.

"How did you find me? We had the adoption sealed," she replied.

"Are you Natalie's mom?" I asked.

"I am." She paused. "I apologize. I'm so rude; please come in. We can talk more comfortably inside if you would like," she said as she opened the door wider.

"I would love to," I said with a half-smile.

We sat and talked for a long time, a couple hours at least. She was very friendly and inviting. Even though I didn't get to meet my biological mother, I at least got to meet my grandmother, Mary, and I learned a lot. The news was a little overwhelming, to say the least. My mother died in a car accident. They were moving and starting a new life. A lot of tears were shed as we talked. My poor grandmother has been through a lot in her life. I could tell she had a tremendously hard time telling me about my biological father.

He raped my biological mother for years during her adolescent years and she ended up getting pregnant with twins. And that's the reason for the closed adoption. Natalie was only fifteen at the time and my grandmother felt she was too young and didn't want to be reminded of the rape every day. Natalie's father, and my grandmother's husband, Elliott, committed suicide. From what I gathered, he was having an affair with his secretary from work and his friend watched over Natalie while he was cheating on his wife, my grandmother, while she was away on business trips. My grandmother didn't suspect him of infidelity. She was under the impression that Natalie and her father were getting plenty of father-daughter bonding time. My poor grandmother lost her husband, her daughter, and two grandchildren all in less than a year.

I told my grandmother about my life and about my daughter's condition and why I was able to get the closed adoption unsealed. My grandmother said she would like to meet my parents and my daughter before we headed back to Virginia. She made it very clear that she hoped I wouldn't "be a stranger" and would keep in touch. She also mentioned she would contact as many people as possible and do some research into her family history as well.

Now that I have found out quite a bit about my biological parents. It's time I spend some serious time trying to find Julia's biological family now.

I kept in contact with my grandmother on a weekly basis. Mary said she would get a petition from the courthouse and try to get the adoption records of my sister unsealed, due to Isabella's condition. Besides, she mentioned that after finally getting to meet me, she wanted to meet my twin sister. I was interested in finding out about her too, but my main concern was finding out about Julia's biological family.

Without Julia's parents alive to help me find the state Julia was adopted in, I had come to a dead end. I reached out to Julia's Aunt and Uncle, but they didn't have any helpful answers. They hadn't the slightest clue that Julia was even adopted. They said Janessa was pregnant, or at least she said she was. They saw her in the early stages of the pregnancy when women don't show. They came to see baby Julia for the first time a couple months after she was born and never suspected she was anything but a blood relative.

***

My grandmother called with amazing news. She was able to get a hold of my biological father, Joseph Anderson, on death row for killing two men in prison. She had gone to visit him at the South Dakota State Penitentiary in Sioux Falls. He told her that while serving his ten-year sentence for raping Natalie, he was attacked numerous times by inmates leaving him with several broken bones, bruises, and cuts. He was even raped on numerous occasions. The guy was tortured the entire ten years. He was almost beaten to death, more than once. The other inmates wanted him to suffer for what he did to my mother. Men, even in prison, don't like a man who sexually preys on children.

During the end of his original sentence, he ended up killing two men with a shank. He's been waiting on death row for fifteen years. He's scheduled for execution in less than a week. I kept hearing her words repeating over and over again, like a broken record player. "He has the same blood type as Isabella and has agreed to be a living donor for her heart transplant."

This was the best news I'd heard in such a long time that I broke down in tears of joy. I'd been so scared for my baby girl, so afraid she was going to be taken from me that I couldn't eat or sleep. I'd lost twenty pounds in the last two months and looked sick. This was a dream come true! And to think, my piece of shit biological father was actually going to do something good for this family. But I can definitely say, after hearing what he'd been through for the last twenty-five years, I think he had been punished enough for what he did to my mother. But most importantly, he agreed to donate his heart to Isabella, and for that, I can't thank him enough.

DEVASTATING DISCOVERY

Isabella's heart transplant was scheduled today. The heart had to be delivered within six hours. Our only option was to transport Isabella's donor heart via helicopter from Sioux Falls, South Dakota to the transplant center in Roanoke, Virginia where the surgery would be performed.

***

The operation went without hiccup. The surgeon said it generally takes three to six months to fully recover from the surgery and Isabella would need to be in the ICU for two to three days, although it all depended on her overall recovery. Once she was stable, she would be transferred to a private room in the intermediate ICU. She would have physical and occupational therapists working with her to build up her strength and stamina before they would release her to go home. At that point, she would have several follow-up appointments at the transplant center. Testing included blood work, echocardiograms, electrocardiograms, and heart biopsies.

My grandmother came to visit us once Isabella was transferred to intermediate ICU. She brought a cute teddy bear holding a heart and a bunch of balloons. Once visiting hours were over, I had my grandmother follow me back to my house and welcomed her to stay with me until she flew back home to South Dakota.

She came bearing more good news. "Trevor, I just wanted you to know that I was able to get your sister's closed adoption unsealed," Mary claimed.

"That's wonderful news, Grandma," I replied.

"I was able to obtain her adoptive parents names and address. But when I went to check if they still lived there, the man who answered the door said his family had lived in that house for twenty years and he didn't know anyone by that name."

"How will we ever find them?" I questioned.

"I'm not sure. Some families move a lot, of course, and so it might be hard to track them down. Since the adoption was closed, it's not necessary for them to update any records when they move. Unfortunately, this might be the dead end to our search. They could be anywhere," Mary said, obviously bummed.

"We could Google their names. We might get lucky. If there's lots of people with the same names, at least we can try to narrow it down. You'd be surprised the information you can get on people nowadays just by typing their name into a search engine. It's actually kind of scary if you ask me, but in this case, it might help us find my sister," I replied.

"It doesn't hurt to try," Mary exclaimed.

"Let me grab my laptop so we can search their names," I said, then ran to my bedroom. In no time, I was back sitting next to my grandmother, anxiously waiting for the names so we could get this party started. "Grandma, I need their names."

"Oh, yes, that might help. Sorry, but I've forgotten already so let me find it. I wrote their names down here somewhere. Yes, here it is. Their names are Alex and Janessa Hendricks," Mary confirmed.

I froze. This can't be happening. Oh…My…God! I instantly felt sick to my stomach. Without saying a word, I bolted out of the room and ran to the bathroom as fast as I could, where I violently vomited up my dinner. I sat down in front of the toilet as sweat was dripping down my forehead. How could this be? I thought my life was perfect with Julia. We had such a strong connection and I wanted to spend the rest of my life with her. But I married my twin sister and had a baby with her. I threw up again. This is so morally wrong. We're going to be severally punished for this. But neither one of us had a clue, I reminded myself. It's not our fault.

For one, Julia didn't even know she was adopted. Second, she had a different birthday then mine. How could that be? Unless, Alex and Janessa celebrated her birthday the day the adoption was final, and she came home with them. I supposed that strong connection we felt was not the world drawing us in to each other because we were destined to be together or soul mates. It was because we were twins and that's why we had such a strong connection. I started heaving again, but I had nothing left in my stomach. How am I going to explain this to my parents, to my grandmother or my daughter when she is old enough to understand? I began heaving again.

Then I thought of our wedding day, of the unexplained storm that erupted out of nowhere and then vanished as fast as it had begun. It was a sign from God, warning us that he was angry with the union. Julia's parents were killed in a car accident shortly after we met that summer. Maybe Julia's parents' lives ended because of the lie they lived. Julia died during childbirth and Isabella's heart condition was a result of our unforgiveable union. I've always been a true believer that everything happens for a reason, even if we don't understand it at first. But now all this tragedy was starting to make sense.

We were being punished.

What will happen to this family next?

I heard a light tapping on the door. "Trevor, are you alright?" Mary asked in a quiet, shaky voice. "I'm okay, Grandma. I'll be right out. Just give me a minute," I replied, trying to collect my thoughts.

When I finally sat down with my grandmother, we had the most difficult conversation I ever had to endure. I revealed the horrible, unforgiveable revelation that my deceased wife was the granddaughter that she would never get to meet and my twin sister. My grandmother's reaction was surprising. I thought she would cry uncontrollably, but instead she sat there frozen in shock for just a minute or two, then gave me a big hug to comfort me. She kept trying to reassure me that everything was going to be okay and that it was not our fault, that we didn't know. In fact, she took the blame. She said, if she hadn't of made Natalie give us up for adoption in the first place, Natalie would probably still be alive, and so would Julia's adoptive parents, and Julia. And that's when the tears started flowing for us both.

***

My grandmother stayed with me for a week as we continued to bond and build a relationship that was missing for the first twenty-five years of my life. Mary was an amazing woman and had been through hell and back. Because she was very kind and comforting, she made even the terrible news I had just received much more tolerable by just being around. But after she left, we continued to keep in contact once a week.

***

Mary finally decided there was nothing keeping her in South Dakota anymore. She wanted to move closer to us so she could see Isabella grow up, since she missed that with Julia and me. I offered her the guest house on our property since she was retirement age and I could keep an eye on her. She would also be close by for all the holidays and birthdays. I'm so glad I found my grandmother, the closest thing to my actual mother, whom I never got to meet. She was able to tell me all about my mother and showed me lots of pictures.

My grandmother informed me that she was sending a copy of the newspaper article regarding the execution of my biological father, Joseph Anderson. She asked that I call her after I read the article to discuss some information that connected my biological father to someone who impacted her life severely. The article stated: "Joseph Anderson was imprisoned on June 6, 1993 for numerous counts of molesting and raping an eleven-year-old girl over three years, which resulted in the victim getting pregnant with twins at the age of fourteen. After giving up the babies in a closed adoption, the victim and her mother were subsequently involved in a car crash that resulted in the death of the victim only days after childbirth. Joseph Anderson served ten years in Sioux Falls State Penitentiary where he was brutally attacked on several occasions. Joseph killed two men just weeks before his scheduled release. He was executed on March 9, 2018. Only three people have been executed in the State of South Dakota since capital punishment was reinstated in 1979. Joseph Anderson donated his heart to his granddaughter, who shared an extremely rare blood type, AB-, which according to American Red Cross, is present in only 1% of Caucasians. His granddaughter was on the donor list for a transplant. Is this his saving grace? Or will Joseph Anderson be doomed even after death? Joseph is survived by his father Jack Anderson, his mother Janet Anderson, his brother Jonathan Anderson, sister Jennifer Olsen, half-brother Lance Conrad, his son Trevor Williams, and his granddaughter Isabella Williams."

I set the newspaper down and called my grandmother like she had asked. The phone rang a few times before Mary picked up.

"Hi, Grandma. I just finished reading the newspaper article you sent me."

"The interesting news I wanted to share with you is that Joseph's half-brother is Lance Conrad," Mary said.

"Who's Lance Conrad?" I asked.

"My parents were killed by a drunk driver when I was twelve. The man who killed my parents was from a wealthy, powerful family in South Dakota. The charges were dropped to vehicular manslaughter, and he was sentenced to ten years in prison with all but thirty-six months suspended. After only serving thirty months, just two and a half years, he was released. That man was Lance Conrad!" my grandmother explained. "Both Lance Conrad and Joseph Anderson have destroyed my life beyond repair." Mary began to weep.

I wanted to reach through the phone and give my grandmother a hug. I couldn't imagine the emotions this news must be stirring up, having to relive her parents death and the horrible things that happened to her daughter all over again. I wanted to say the right words to comfort her, but all that would pass through my lips was: "I'm so sorry, Grandma."

THE CURSE

I flew to South Dakota to help my grandmother pack up all her belongings to move to Virginia to be close to us. My grandmother picked me up at the airport in Sioux Falls, and on our ninety-minute drive back to her house we had an interesting conversation.

"Now I know why this family is cursed. Why bad things always seem to happen to us!" she exclaimed. "I was up late one night because I couldn't sleep, which happens often when you suffer from chronic insomnia as I do. I was going through some old boxes of my parents' belongings in the attic when I stumbled across an antique lock box. It looked like it had to be at least a hundred years old, if not more, and I had to break it open. I was quite nervous to look inside because just touching it gave me the most dreadful feeling that chilled me to the bone. But my curiosity would not let it be, even with the evil aura that seemed to protect it. I don't know why I never tried opening it before because I've had it in my possession since my parents passed away. It's been up in my attic since your grandfather, Elliott, and I moved into this house more than forty years ago, and I just forgot about it. After reading my mother's diary years after she died, I found out the antique box was given to her by her grandmother, Margaret. My mother described Margaret as a very strange woman who gave her the creeps. It was in my mom's possession since her grandmother passed away, but she never opened it."

Mary squirmed uncomfortably in the driver's seat. "She described the box as feeling wicked and possessed, and so she feared opening it. She said it gave her a gut-wrenching feeling. Margaret told my mother when she gave her the box that an angel would be born who was the only one who could break the curse that has been on this family for generations. My mom thought Margaret was delusional and she tried to bury the box far away from our family, but it mysteriously appeared back in the house only hours after she buried it. This completely freaked my mother out, and so she tried burning it in the fire pit at our house. But when the fire stopped smoldering several hours later, the box was not damaged. It was in perfect condition, untouched by the fire. This was the last entry in my mother's diary."

Mary wiped a tear, then turned from the highway onto a residential street. "Only a couple weeks after the incident, my parents were killed by a drunk driver, and I have always wondered if she was punished for trying to destroy the box." Mary's tone grew thick with resolve now. "If there is a curse on this family, and it sure seems to me that there is given all the death and suffering, and if the curse can be broken, I need to do something about it. I opened the box and there was a book inside, a diary, and in between the pages was a folded-up piece of paper. I unfolded the paper, but the note was in a different language and so I couldn't understand what it said. Instead, I read the diary entry that the paper seemed to mark its place. The diary belonged to my great grandmother, Margaret. The entry said, a crazy woman approached her on the street in London, dressed in all black, her face hidden by a hooded cloak. She stated in a stern voice, that Margaret would be punished for marrying Aaron Kosminski and that any child born of them, and all their descendants, thereafter, would be tortured by a curse of torment. She claimed that an angel would be born into the family, and that angel, would be the only one that could break the curse. She handed her a folded piece of paper, turned and walked away, disappearing into the darkness. Margaret also claimed in the diary entry that the woman who approached her was also known for performing witchcraft in London."

"Wow, Grandma. That's really creepy!" I replied nervously.

"We are descendants of Aaron Kosminski!" Mary blurted out.

"Who is Aaron Kosminski? I've never heard of him before."

"Have you heard of the notorious Jack the Ripper?" Mary asked.

"Yes, of course. Why?" I asked.

"Jack the Ripper was the name given to an unidentified serial killer in London during the late 19th century. He is believed to have killed five women. The legend of Jack the Ripper is one of the most enduring murder mysteries of all time—the real identity of the killer was never discovered. The gruesome nature of the murders terrified people. The police never found a definite clue leading to the identity of the murderer but managed to develop a list of suspects. The identity of the killer puzzled detectives for well over a century. Even though Jack the Ripper was never charged with the murders, many sources suggested that Jack the Ripper was a 23-year-old Polish immigrant named Aaron Kosminski. Aaron Kosminski is my great-great grandfather! We are descendants of Jack the Ripper!"

I just sat there froze, not knowing what to say. This was a lot of information to wrap my head around. I finally was able to speak. "Grandma, what are we going to do?"

"I sent the letter to an old friend of mine to be translated. I got it back in the mail this morning before I came to pick you up at the airport. Her letter is sitting unopened on the counter at my house. We will have to read it when we get back," Mary said with a shaky voice.

When we got to Mary's house, she opened the letter and read the translation out load: "Aaron Kosminski, a monster who has brutally mutilated many victims, was never punished for his crimes. So I am manifesting a curse on all his kinfolk for many generations to come to cause them harm, severe afflictions, sickness and even death so that some form of cosmic restitution for Kosminski's victims can be achieved. The only way this curse can be broken is by an angel born unto this family by a miracle. This angel has to repeat this spell during a new moon at midnight while burning sage and the curse will be broken." Mary continued, *"In the names of my ancestors, my gods, and myself, I call upon thee, oh creatures of Earth and Water. Come forth, cleanse the descendants of Aaron Kosminski of all evil and magicks and restore us to balance and health. By our wills combined, so mote it be."* Mary paused for a moment, then with a look of confusion added, "For some odd reason this spell sounds too familiar, like I've heard it before."

"Grandma, who is this angel she is talking about?" I replied.

"She must be referring to my sister, Angel. My mother wasn't supposed to have any more children, but by a miracle she got pregnant again. And my parents called her their Angel of Hope," Mary replied.

"Where is Angel? Do you still talk to her? Please tell me she is still alive."

"Angel has been in the nursing home in Estelline for over a year now. I visit her twice a month. She was diagnosed with Alzheimer's. She still remembers me at least, but her condition is worsening," Mary exclaimed.

"Can we visit her, to see if she will recite the spell so this curse can once and for all be broken and we can live out our lives in peace?" I pleaded.

"We are in luck. There is a new moon tomorrow evening, but unfortunately visiting hours are over at 9:00. The spell specifies it can only be recited at midnight for it to work."

"We have to figure something out. We need this curse broken, Grandma."

***

It was fifteen minutes before midnight when we arrived at the Estelline Nursing and Care Center. We had come to visit Angel earlier in the day and told her about the curse and all the findings we discovered. There was a thick blanket of fog this evening, making it hard to see as we snuck up to her window on the west side of the building and knocked lightly on the glass. It was no easy task, but we managed to get the aged Angel through the window, and then the three of us walked to a secluded area some distance from the facility and took out the sage and the spell to break the curse on this family. Mary lit the sage while we all held hands in a circle, and then Angel recited the spell:

"In the names of my ancestors, my gods, and myself, I call upon thee, oh creatures of Earth and Water. Come forth, cleanse the descendants of Aaron Kosminski of all evil and magicks, and restore us to balance and health. By our wills combined, so mote it be."

As we stood there in silence waiting for something miraculous to happen, a huge gust of wind circled around us while we stood in the eye of it, leaves and dust whipping around us like a tornado for several minutes. The wind slowly faded and then disappeared above us, leaving a clear sky filled with thousands of bright stars dancing in the moonlight.

I felt as if a heavy weight had been lifted off my shoulders and was replaced with peace and harmony. The lessons in life may have tattooed my very soul, but I have learned to let go of what I cannot change by not letting pain hold me captive, to rise from the ashes of shattered dreams and to spread my wings in these bittersweet moments and fly against all odds.

E. A. Owen

Twisted Karma Publishing

Tragic Mercy: Book I (2019)

Suffocating Secrets: Tragic Mercy Book II
(2019)

Tragic Mercy Book III
(Coming 2020)

A Reader's Journal (2019) Over 100-pages to
keep track of all the books you read, book reviews,
favorite books and authors, book wishlist, and more.

Author Website: eaowenbooks.com
Facebook.com/eaowenbooks